Rockett's World

WHAT KIND OF FRIEND ARE YOU?

Read more about

Rockett's World
in:
#1 WHO CAN YOU
TRUST?
#3 ARE WE THERE
YET?

Rockett's World

WHAT KIND OF FRIEND ARE YOU?

Lauren Day

SCHOLASTIC INC.

New York Toronto London Auckland Sydney
Mexico City New Delhi Hong Kong

ISBN 0-439-06312-4

12 11 10 9 8 7 6 5 4 3   9/9 0 1 2 3 4/0

Printed in the U.S.A.   40
First Scholastic printing, August 1999

Acknowledgments

The author never has to wonder what kind of friends she has: totally, the best! Among them, and especially in Rockett's World are: Kate Egan, editor deluxe; Madalina Stefan, artist extraordinaire; Annie McDonnell, production princess; Maria Barbo, indispensable assistant to the stars; Craig Walker, the *boss* boss; and of course, Jean Feiwel, genius visionary. I am in debt to one and all.

Rockett's World

WHAT KIND OF FRIEND ARE YOU?

Nicole   Miko   Stephanie   Rockett   Ruben

Bo

Whitney

Nakili

Cleve

Arnold

INTRODUCTION

What's up? I'm Rockett — Rockett Movado. Okay, weird name, I know. My parents came up with it. I actually like it, but then again, I've had thirteen years to get used to it.

What I'm not totally used to — yet — is my new school. Our family moves around a lot. My dad's an inventor and my mom's a collage artist, and they both believe in being open to new experiences. We just settled into our home a few months ago, so I'm still the new girl at Whistling Pines Junior High School. I like meeting new people, but there *are* certain drawbacks: the biggest being not having a best friend yet.

At least I've met everyone in my grade — that's eighth. When I first got there, all the kids said, "Whistling Pines is the best place to be." The jury's still out on that one, but I did get off to a rockin' start with a lot of kids there — especially this girl Jessie, who I've sort of bonded with. And Miko and Nakili. Even though they're part of a clique, they've been totally nice to me.

And, okay, a not-too-cool start with some others. In the very first weeks of school, I found out this mega-secret about a certain snobby person. The same one who played a mean trick on me. Some of the decisions I made worked out. Others turned out to be humongo mistakes. Big-time trauma-rama followed!

But I believe in second chances — even third, fourth, and fifth, when necessary. If time stopped right now, I would say everything's pretty cool with all the kids at Whistling Pines.

I'm buckling my backpack and heading out the door to school right now, as a matter of fact. Come with me? Let's see what develops.

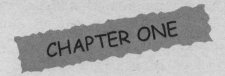
CHAPTER ONE

"Heads up! In*coming!*"

Luckily, Rockett heard the warning just in time and ducked. The Frisbee went whizzing *by* her head, instead of *into* it. She didn't have to look up to know who the culprits were.

Cleve and Max, Whistling Pines Junior High's officially classified cutups, were at it again — before the school day had even begun! She zoned in on the tall blond half of the goof-troop.

"Thanks for the radar alert, Cleve, but . . . um . . . don't you think you better put that away before Principal Herrera confiscates it?"

It was Monday morning and the three were among the first students to arrive at school, where, indoors, Frisbee tosses were on the "don't even think about it" list.

Freckle-faced Max, shorter than his bud by, like, a foot, was clutching the Frisbee now. He answered for both of them. "Thanks for caring, new girl, but since our favorite authority figure isn't in the vicinity just now . . ."

" . . . and *doesn't* have a homing device on us," Cleve chimed in.

". . . we'll take our chances," Max finished.

Rockett put her hands on her hips and tilted her head.

"Whatever, you guys. But from what I hear, one more infraction and you're headed down detention road."

"Oooh, detention! Mommy! I'm scared! Can I bring my blankee?" Cleve quipped as he took the Frisbee and motioned for Max to go back for another pass.

Rockett rolled her eyes. Sometimes these two could actually be funny. This wasn't one of those times. "So, anyway," she asked, not really wanting the convo to end just yet, "when do I get to stop being called 'new girl'? I've been here almost two months, and I know *everyone*. Some people a lot more than I'd like to."

Cleve had to laugh. He knew exactly what Rockett was referring to. "Until someone else moves here, Ms. Rockett Movado — tag, you're it! So roll with it — come on, have some fun. Go back to where Max is standing, I'll toss you one."

Rockett hesitated. *This is so against the rules — I better not. But they're being so friendly, really including me. That would be kind of cool. Besides, they're not hurting anyone. And I don't want them to think I'm some Goody Two-shoes. I'll . . .*

Rockett's train of thought was derailed by the *click-clack* of chunky heels coming briskly down the school corridor. A quick glance in the direction of the noise confirmed her suspicion: Principal Herrera.

Rockett opened her mouth to warn Cleve, but she was too late. He'd already flung the Frisbee toward Max. Just as the principal materialized.

She was *not* amused. Eyes flashing at Cleve, she challenged, "Pop quiz, Mr. Goodstaff! Name three things that are against the rules at Whistling Pines."

Cleve tried to joke his way out of it. "Uh, that would be . . . uh . . . well, homicide . . . cheating . . . and boys in the girls' locker room." He shot Mrs. Herrera his most charming, boyish grin.

She wasn't buying it. But she did soften a bit. "I'll do you a favor, Cleveland. Since the hallway is almost empty and you didn't hurt anyone, I'll let you off with a warning. But one more rule-breaker, and you will report to my office for detention."

Cleve let out a major sigh of relief as the principal focused on Max and added, "This means you, too, Mr. Diamond. I'll take the Frisbee now."

The boys didn't argue, but handed over the offending flying object. The minute Mrs. Herrera walked away, Rockett noted, "Close call, Cleve."

Confidence was not something Cleve lacked. Ever. His eyes twinkled mischievously. "No big. Watch, we'll have it back by the end of the day." Just then, he did a quick one-eighty. "Anyway, Rockett, speaking of *calls* — close, or otherwise — have you made *yours* yet about Nicole's proposition?"

Rockett was only a little surprised Cleve knew about it. He and Max, after all, *were* in Nicole's posse. The Ones, they called themselves. Everyone else called them popular — as in, *way* popular. Their leader, Nicole Whittaker, was running for class president. And just a few days ago, she'd actually invited Rockett to be on their ticket.

5

"I haven't come close to deciding," Rockett answered Cleve honestly. Nicole's proposition required a kind of major decision.

The three set out in the direction of their lockers. "Well," Max advised, "if I were you, I'd hurry up and decide to join up with us. Because this is going to be one fun ride, right to the top of Whistling Pines student government. We, The Ones party, *will* rule the school!"

"We? Are you on the ticket?" Rockett asked.

"Nah, I work strictly behind the scenes. Diamond's the name — strategy's the game!" Max puffed his chest out proudly. Pointing at Cleve, he added, "There's your treasurer, though."

Rockett's eyebrows shot up. The whole class election thing hadn't ramped up. Yet it seemed as if Nicole's team was already in place — almost. "Really? So if Nicole's running for president, and you're going for treasurer, I guess other people have already committed . . . ?"

Cleve responded coolly as he pulled a yo-yo out of the deep side pocket of his cargo pants and started to Rock the Cradle with it. "Sure. Steph's on for secretary."

He meant Stephanie Hollis, charter member of The Ones. Stephanie had a sweet and caring side, but the way she always agreed with everything Nicole said gave the girl a major demerit in Rockett's mind.

"Which leaves the position of vice president open," Cleve was saying. "That could be you, Rockett — if you seize the moment and accept."

"And if I don't . . . ?" Rockett trusted Nicole about as far as Little Red Riding Hood trusted the big bad wolf. And besides, she was sure Nicole had a backup in mind.

"If you go all duh-head and decline, it will be —" Cleve started.

"*Her,*" Max interrupted, nodding at the approaching form of Whitney Weiss. Blond, curly-haired Whitney noticed the trio and, from a distance, waved.

By that time, Max, Cleve, and Rockett had reached the hallway where the eighth-grade lockers were lined up. Whitney's locker was right next to Rockett's. A second before she was upon them, Cleve leaned over and whispered in Rockett's ear — answering the very question that had leaped to the front of her brain.

"Don't say anything to Whitney about the election! She doesn't know yet that Nicole asked you — our fearless leader likes to keep her options open."

Rockett's eyes went wide. She hurriedly whispered back, "So Whitney thinks *she's* on the ticket as vice president — I mean, *automatically*, because she's part of The Ones?"

Cleve didn't answer verbally. Instead, he formed a pistol with his forefinger and thumb and pointed at Rockett, indicating, *You got that right.*

"What's up with the whispering?" Whitney hadn't missed the exchange. "Are we gossiping about someone? Someone I know?"

Whitney despised being left out — of anything. Rockett felt a pang of guilt. *Okay, so Whitney's a total One, and sometimes a total phony — but she does have a mind of her own, sometimes. Unlike Stephanie, she doesn't always agree blindly with Nicole. In some ways, I really like her. And I definitely wouldn't want to hurt her. . . .*

But before Rockett could say anything, Max teased, "You! They're gossiping about you, Whitney. Cleve just told Rockett your real first name!"

Whitney rolled her eyes. "Headline news. Whatever. Don't you two have elsewhere to be — like your own lockers, since the homeroom bell is minutes away? And we all know how much mirror time Cleve requires!"

Rockett had to giggle. Although Whitney's taunt didn't seem to bother Cleve, it was full-on bull's-eye. Cleve *was* pretty self-absorbed. He'd even hung a mirror on the inside of his locker door. But his perpetual good nature — and okay, he was cute, athletic, and charming — kept him popular.

Cleve and Max sauntered down the hallway, which was quickly filling up with students. Whitney turned her attention to Rockett. "So, how was your weekend?" Only Whitney didn't really want to know. It was the kind of question meant to lead into her telling about hers — she didn't even give Rockett a second to answer, but continued, "Mine *so* did not kick. I was all, 'I'm going to the mall with Nic and Stef,' but my father was like, 'Don't even think about it.'"

"Why not?" Rockett asked, surprised. Whitney acted

8

like she always got her way. Her clothes were pretty trendy, anyway — just like Nicole's and Stephanie's and the rest of their group's. "Does he think you're spending too much time shopping?" Rockett guessed.

"Not *enough* time — studying, that is." Whitney's back was turned to Rockett as she fished inside her locker. "There it is! I knew I hadn't lost that stupid book." When she turned around, she was holding a copy of *The Taming of the Shrew*. The book she should have had at home, but had obviously left at school.

Rockett got it, instantly. Whitney had messed up a previous assignment, too, by not reading *Tuck Everlasting*. For that unit only — because of this beginning-of-the-semester scheduling screwup — she was in Rockett's language arts class. And would have gotten in trouble when the teacher called on her, but Rockett had slyly helped her out.

"GPA meltdown again?" Rockett asked sympathetically.

Whitney whined, "I hate this dumb class. Why can't we ever have any books written in English?"

Rockett stifled a giggle. "Shakespeare is English, circa the sixteenth century, anyway. It just takes some getting used to."

"Who has the time or energy to get used to this stuff? Not-ith me-ith!"

This time, Rockett did giggle — although Whitney's attempt at mocking Shakespeare was majorly lame.

"Well," she noted, "it *is* part of the dad job requirement to see that you *make* time for studying."

Whitney frowned. "My dad acts like grades are all that matters. He even dangles my GPA in front of me like . . ." She never finished the sentence, because just then, Stephanie whisked by, so quickly that her long earrings swung. Without breaking stride, she grabbed Whitney's elbow and announced, "Nic's calling a quick meeting by her locker — come on!"

Whitney slammed her locker shut and, in a flash, she and Stephanie were down the hall.

Leaving Rockett by herself.

Determined not to be hurt — after all, she wasn't in their clique, like she'd even *want* to be! — she opened her backpack and put the books for her afternoon classes in her locker. It only took a second. And Rockett wasn't into checking and rechecking her look in a mirror.

Instead, she checked her watch. A few minutes remained till homeroom. She paused. *I feel kind of weird standing here all alone. Everyone's got someone to talk to. I did, too, up until a minute ago! Maybe I'll go find Jessie. Or I could look for Miko and Nakili — I wonder why I don't see them? Being solo is okay. It leaves my options open. But it also leaves me feeling . . . like it's my first day all over again.*

Confession Session

Touchdown! I called it Day One. Did I not tell everyone that Rockett Movado is okay? No babe, but cute, in an offbeat way. But, ha-ha, I think she should wear a shirt that says, I SURVIVED HURRICANE NICOLE. Man, Nic dealt her some low blows! First, that phony note supposedly written by Ruben. Then, from what I hear, the sleepover got way out of hand and Rockett ran out. Okay, maybe I had a part in the note thing — I knew it was bogus — but I wasn't even like the driver of the getaway car. I was just a bystander. Guilty by association only. But what guy *wouldn't* want to be associated with Nicole? Anyway, there's obviously some truce between Rockett and Nicole. Or why would Nic have asked her to be on *our* team for the elections? Life is good.

Rockett in
the mix is
shaking things
up — me like, me like!
Especially since the redhead
is already tight with a certain
other girl. And maybe I want
to get to know *other* girl
better. Can't let on yet,
since *other* girl isn't exactly
a One, or anywhere close.
But if Rockett comes with
us, good chance *other* girl
will follow. And then,
who knows? But until
everything falls into
place, I keep
my . . . interest . . .
on the
down-low.

What's up with the whispering between Cleve and Rockett? He's done nothing but tease her since she got here. But . . . could he . . . *like* her now? That would be . . . interesting enough to spread around! If only I had the time. How lame is it that I don't have one second to gossip? But I am soooo stressed. I wish my dad hadn't given me that ultimatum, and just let me do what I want to do. I am in eighth grade! I have *stuff*! To deal with! Deal-ith wi-ith!!

CHAPTER TWO

Flipping her backpack securely over both shoulders, Rockett strode purposefully over to Jessie's locker. It was open, and her sunny-side-up girlfriend was behind the door. Jessie wasn't alone. Darnetta was right there.

Rockett had nothing against 'Netta, as Jessie called her; in fact, in some ways she had been incredibly supportive during Rockett's trauma-rama with Nicole. But for some reason, Rockett hadn't really clicked with Darnetta. That Jessie *did* sometimes made Rockett feel like a third wheel.

"Hey, guys," Rockett greeted them both cheerily.

In a flash, Jessie closed her locker and shot Rockett a big smile. "What's up, Rockett? 'Netta and I were just rewinding Saturday. That blading adventure was awesome!"

Rockett glowed. Getting the three of them together had been her idea. Jessie was *so* into the idea of the three of them being best friends. Rockett wasn't so sure, but figured an afternoon with them could be cool. For the most part, it was. Even if Jessie and Darnetta had gotten off on this computer-talk jag that made Rockett feel a little left out.

Suddenly, Jessie lowered her voice. "Listen, you guys.

14

I have something to show you. Someone gave me a gift, I guess. It was in my mailbox on Sunday morning. I don't know who it's from."

Rockett was intrigued.

"Describe!" Darnetta commanded, equally interested.

Jessie glanced around. "Not now. Let's do it at lunch, okay? I mean, it might be from someone who could walk by at any moment."

"Show-and-tell at Lunch Table Six!" Darnetta declared. "See you there — you, too, Rockett, right?"

"I wouldn't miss it!"

The bell rang and the three headed to homeroom together. No seats had been assigned exactly, but the eighth graders pretty much grabbed the same ones every day. Rockett wasn't at all bummed that hers was next to Ruben.

Ruben Rosales had her vote for coolest boy at Whistling Pines. He had lots going for him. A) He wasn't in any clique, so that made him an independent thinker. Huge plus. B) He was big-time into his music, an artistic quality Rockett totally related to. C) He was friendly — to everyone. Which is exactly how Rockett intended to be. And okay, if she had to admit it, there was . . . D) Ruben was crazy-cute.

And right now, leaning over, he was talking to her. "So how was your weekend, new girl? Jammin' in the fun zone or all nose-to-the-grindstone?"

"A little of both. I went blading on Saturday, but spent most of Sunday on homework. How about you?"

Ruben played air guitar and cocked his head. "Had to grab study breaks between rehearsals. The band is tightening up."

"Are you playing somewhere soon?" Rockett asked.

"No gigs lined up, but before you know it, it'll be party season and Rebel Angels will be good to go."

Just then, Mr. Baldus (who Rockett had decided was sort of a combination of homeroom teacher and ringmaster) called the class to attention. Baldus always spoke in exclamation points! And he was totally stuck in some generation not their own.

"Greetings, my hippest bunch of hepcats ever! You've set your radios on WPHC — that's Whistling Pines Homeroom Class, for the anagram-challenged! So mute the chitchat, turn up the volume, and listen for the hits — when you hear your name, give a shout-out and let us know you are *in the house!*"

On his last few words, Miko, Nakili, and Dana dashed in — just under the late bell. Studious Miko, who prided herself on a blemish-free record, didn't want to take any chances getting a tardy.

"Sorry we're late, Mr. Baldus," she breathlessly explained, sliding in to her seat. "We actually got to school early. We had an important meeting in the art classroom."

They did? Why didn't they include me? Even though they're a clique, the CSGs, Miko and Nakili have been totally friendly to me. Even if I still don't know what CSG stands for! I bet sourpuss Dana insisted on leaving me out.

Maybe I'll pass Nakili a note asking her what the meeting was about. But . . . maybe not. What if that puts her on the spot? But at least I'd know . . .

Because Rockett's mind had wandered, when Mr. Baldus called her name, she didn't hear it — the first time, that is.

"Rockett-to-the-moon-girl, I know you're here somewhere — come in for a landing!"

Embarrassment alert! Rockett couldn't help blushing as she mumbled, "Here! Sorry, I was . . ."

"Off in some parallel universe?" Baldus guessed good-naturedly. "Well, reenter the earth's atmosphere, because it's pretty groovy down here. And about to get groovier!" With that, Mr. Baldus turned his back to the class to write something on the blackboard: CLASS ELECTIONS! He underlined it twice.

Baldus immediately launched into what sounded like a huge run-on sentence explaining what student government was: "A chance to have a voice in the running of your school!"

And what it wasn't: "A popularity contest."

He described the positions to be filled: "Class president, vice president, secretary, and treasurer." And when the deadline for applying for candidacy was: the end of the week. "Sign-up sheets are in Mrs. Herrera's office and, as always, all candidates are welcome to toss their hats into the ring. . . ."

"Including non- and subhumans?" Max piped up as he shot a rubber band in the direction of Arnold Zeitbaum.

Rockett cringed. It always bugged her when one kid was picked on, and now that she'd gotten to know Arnold a little, Max's taunts were so not funny. Okay, so Arnold was dermatologically challenged. And a science-head who talked in some medieval geek language sometimes. Still, that didn't make the teasing right.

Luckily, Max's aim was off: Neither his rubber band nor his zinger hit the mark. Arnold merely snorted, and then, surprisingly, raised his hand. Defiantly, he asked Mr. Baldus, "Where did you say the sign-ups were?"

Baldus beamed. "Piled high in the principal's office, Mr. Zeitbaum." Then Baldus did an about-face, zeroing in on Max. "Which is where *you* may find yourself, if you're not careful, Mr. Diamond — for detention. Which brings me to my final point. There *are* some people who will be excluded from running. That would be anyone with three or more detentions, anyone caught cheating, anyone with an average below C, and anyone who's been expelled. But that last group wouldn't be here anyway!" Mr. Baldus guffawed at his joke. Alone.

The bell rang. As Rockett gathered her books, she heard Nicole scoff, "I can't believe the Zitbomb's even thinking of running for office. Who'd want to share a zip code with Grandmaster Geek, let alone be on his ticket?"

That ticked off Rockett more than Max picking on Arnold. For the secret she'd found out was that, over the summer, Nicole and Arnold were at the same computer camp — and, because Nicole had been the shunned one there, Arnold saved her from total social annihilation.

He'd been so nice to her — danced with her when no one else asked. An event that Rockett had a picture of. Because Arnold didn't want that story spread, Rockett had, in the end, kept it to herself. But hello? Who was Nicole to keep dissing him?

Now Stephanie jumped on the Nicole dis-wagon. "Maybe the Zitbomb could get Mavis Depew, Girl Weirdo, to run with him. Or should I say, the psychic Depew?"

Confidently, Whitney chimed in, "What's the diff? No one will win against us anyway."

Rockett paid rapt attention to their convo: Would Nicole drop a clue that Whitney — her best friend Whitney — might not even *be* on "their" ticket? But Rockett didn't hear Nicole's reaction. Someone tapped her elbow.

Jessie and Darnetta had fallen into step with her.

"Welcome to your first Whistling Pines class elections, Rockett. They're always a trip," Darnetta said.

"So you've been through others, huh?" Rockett asked.

"Yep, and it's always the same. The popular kids win. So this year? Nicole's team's a gimme."

Rockett gulped. *Should I come out and tell Jessie and Darnetta about Nicole's invitation? I could . . . but then they might tell me how they feel about it. And I don't even know how I feel.* She paused, then went with, "Have either of you guys ever run for anything?"

Darnetta shook her head. "Not my scene. I go my own way."

Jessie shrugged. "I might . . . I mean, I have ideas and stuff. But no one's ever asked me to be on a ticket. And I just wouldn't feel comfortable, you know, organizing my own and asking people. I don't know — maybe next year."

As the girls headed down the hallway to their separate classes, Rockett heard someone call her name.

"Wait up, Rockett! Glad I finally caught you — before first period and, um, in private. Look, I need a favor." It was Whitney, out of breath.

"Sure, Whitney, what's up?"

"Okay, so I'm *totally* tanking in language arts." Whitney held up her hand, anticipating Rockett's response. "Wait, I know what you're thinking: There she goes again! But I'm not asking you to, like, throw me clues in class or anything —"

Whitney seemed *so* nervous! To try and put her at ease Rockett giggled, "You *can't*. Since you changed your schedule, you're not *in* my language arts class anymore. So how can I help you?"

Whitney bit her lip. Instead of looking at Rockett, her eyes darted around the hallway. Finally, she sputtered, "Your class already did *The Taming of the Shrew*, right? And we're, like, just starting it. So would you, like . . . if you have time . . . come over to my house after school and we could go over my reading assignment together? That would so help, and then I could tackle the homework by myself." Now, Whitney made eye contact.

Rockett lit up. "Sure. That'd be cool. So after school, you mean, today?"

Whitney nodded. "My dad picks me up, so we have a ride. And I'm sure he'd drive you home after. Or maybe you could even stay for dinner."

Rockett was psyched as she walked into art class. Okay, so it meant calling her parents and making sure *they* were okay with the change in plans — *and* asking them to tell Mrs. Herrera, so *she* could tell the bus driver that Rockett would not be going home today. All totally doable. *In spite of Whitney's Ones alliance, I still have a good feeling about her. Doing the study-buddy thing with her will be fun.*

But all at once, Rockett's smile dissolved. *Of course, I do feel kind of strange knowing something she doesn't . . . maybe I should tell her. But then she might resent me, and we'd never be friends. Nicole should tell her — that's who she should resent, not me. Oh, well, it's not as if I've even decided to take her place as the vice president candidate on The Ones ticket. I probably won't. Probably.*

Confession Session

Whoo-*hoo!* Things have totally turned around — and I mean that in the bestest way. Rockett and Darnetta are getting closer, so we can all be friends. And I have a secret admirer! I mean, I think so. The note that came with my present said, *Jessie — here's a little gift for you. I saw this and thought of you, and y'know, wanted you to have it. You're a cool girl. Oh, yeah, I go to your school. I'm in your grade.* Is this major or what? Unless it's . . . someone I don't want it to be! I cannot wait to show it to Rockett and 'Netta and see what they think!

What am I gonna do? Ruben and politics — do not mix! But this group asked me to run for vice president. Cool position: two times good. It ups my profile and snags more gigs for Rebel Angels. But . . . there's Ms. Ego-tripper, Nicole, to consider. How would she react if I ran against her? Would she be off me forever? Or respect me more? Like she's all into that other dude. I gotta think about this.

Could I say yes?

That forlorn look, Rockett? It captures you. So maybe we did leave her out — oh, well! Of course . . . I have this sick feeling that, in matters of the election ticket, I might not prevail. But she better watch her step. Rockett Movado cannot invade my turf!

Today is an auspicious day for the Knights of the Purple Orchid! Today I declare the end is near for the reign of Nicole and her pod. Today, duty calls. I will throw down the gauntlet and run for student government! But which of these mortals can possibly understand the workings of a complex and knowing brain — such as my own — to be deemed worthy of joining forces with me? I could ask the Fair RM . . . but if she turned me down, my heart might forever beat . . . no more.

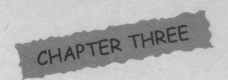

CHAPTER THREE

By the time Rockett got to art class, the CSGs were already there. Ever since the first day, Rockett had sat with them — that is, close to Miko and Nakili, but as far from Dana as possible. Today, she slid into the empty seat by Nakili.

Although it was an elective, the class, taught by Mr. Rarebit — another of Whistling Pines' extremely cool teachers — only admitted the most promising artists in eighth grade. Unofficially, it was called "talent art," and you had to try out for it. Rockett got in easily.

After Mr. Rarebit called the class to order, he announced, "Those of you who are planning to run for class office — and who have completed the project we're on now, surrealism — may use this period to work on any posters, banners, or other art-related projects for your campaign."

Nakili seemed kind of fidgety, like she couldn't wait for Mr. Rarebit to finish talking. The second he did, she pounced on Rockett.

"Got that note you passed me in homeroom, Rockett. Here's wussup with that. We've decided to run for office and we needed to talk to Mr. Rarebit to see if we could use this period to work on our posters."

"Obviously," added Miko, who'd leaned across the desk to join in, "he agreed — as long as everyone else in the class has the same option. That's fair."

Rockett scanned the room. She didn't want to seem *too* anxious to find out more — like who was on their ticket.

"So, since this is my first year here, like, how does it work? In my old school, student government was kind of a big thing: lots of banners, posters, debates, school spirit stuff. Same here?"

Nakili answered, "I'll break it down. About three or four teams run — kids get together with their friends and form a ticket. It's the usual suspects, for the usual reasons. *Some people* do it for status. . . ."

Nakili paused and Rockett knew exactly who she meant: The Ones.

Miko picked up the ball. "Then there are other people — like us — who run because they have actual issues and believe they could make a difference in the school, make it even better than it is."

Rockett was intrigued. "So it *is* a big deal here."

"It could be," Nakili said. "But you know, like anywhere, there's a bunch of kids who never get involved."

"Darnetta mentioned that she's not a joiner," Rockett noted.

"She might not want to be on anyone's ticket, but at least that girl votes her opinions. Unlike some of the others — like those apathetic kids over there . . ." Nakili pointed to the other side of the art room, where Dana had moved, already working on a poster, sitting next to three other kids. Rockett recognized them, but hadn't really talked to any of them ever.

"That's Wolf DuBois," Miko said, in case Rockett didn't know. "He's nice, he's into music and that restaurant his family owns. But he's kind of a loner."

"Kind of cute, too," Nakili couldn't help pointing out.

Miko grinned. "Not that I'm about gossip, but, well, I heard that none other than Nicole Whittaker has a crush on him. But he acts like she's invisible."

Rockett took that in, as Nakili continued, "That other boy? That's Bo Pezanski. He's, like, the detention king here at Whistling Pines — a rebel without a clue. And a loose cannon — completely unpredictable. You never know when he'll suddenly be nice."

"And as for her . . ." Miko motioned toward the one girl at Whistling Pines whom Rockett had so far avoided at all costs. Sharla Norvell. "She's just down on everything."

Secretly, Rockett referred to Sharla as "goth-girl." It was the raccoon-esque eye makeup, combined with her perpetual sneer. Once, Rockett saw her smoking outside the school. Sharla was scary. Worse than Dana. Or even Nicole.

Still, Rockett needed to know more about the whole class election thing. "So have you decided what your issues are?"

"We didn't have to decide, they've been bugging us

28

ever since we got to Whistling Pines in sixth grade," Nakili said.

Miko pulled out a list from her pocket and cleared her throat. "First, the cafeteria food. It reeks. I mean, no veggie meals! Not even barf-a-roni and cheese! Every other school in the district offers a choice for vegetarians — all but us."

"I *know!*" Rockett reacted more vehemently than she'd intended. "That's been a major bummer for me. I am a vegetarian, and if I forget to brown-bag it, then I'm stuck with, like, a salad and yogurt or something."

Nakili and Miko exchanged a look.

Miko continued, "And, it's, like, the new millennium and Whistling Pines could do so much better on environmental issues. I mean, we recycle, but not enough. We need to do separate bins for newspapers, glass, cans. . . ."

"Not to mention a compost heap. There's room behind the track and soccer field," Nakili added.

Rockett could barely contain herself. "I noticed that! In my old school, we did that."

"There's more," Miko continued. "Fun stuff. We support the building of a Rollerblade park adjacent to the school — there's room. And that way we could even have an after-school roller-hockey league."

"And, best of all, for the class trip next month, we're going to advocate going to Washington, D.C. 'Cause, you know, the class gets a say in where we go."

Whomp: There it was. It hit her like a soccer ball to

29

the abs. Rockett totally wanted to be on their team. But . . . they hadn't asked her. And who knew if they planned on it? She fished.

"That's so amazing that you guys are running. All three of you, right?"

Miko pursed her lips. "We would . . . but all three of us . . . can't. Exactly."

Nakili pointed to Dana, on the other side of the room. "She's not eligible."

Rockett's eyebrows arched in surprise. "Why not?"

"Remember what Baldus said about three or more detentions? It carries over from last year, and Dana sort of exceeded the limit."

Rockett nodded. *What a surprise — not!* "But I guess you two are going for president and vice president, then?"

Miko shook her head. "Nakili is a natural leader, so she's running for president. I'd be best at treasurer, keeping track of expenses."

Which left vice president and secretary — but before Rockett could inquire, Nakili answered. "We haven't decided on the other two. Exactly. We did ask one person to run with us for vice president, but this . . . person . . . hasn't answered yet. We're having a quick private meeting in the girls' room between this class and next period to go over our list of possible candidates for secretary."

Miko added, somewhat reluctantly, "It's got to be all three of us — the CSGs — who agree on the candidates. Even if Dana can't be on the ticket, she has an equal vote on who we ask."

Rockett left them to go work on her surrealism project, what Dana jokingly referred to as her "daily dose of Dalí," but she couldn't concentrate. She was so pumped — yet so conflicted.

I'm so right for the CSG ticket! I'm all about every single one of their ideas. Maybe I should just straight out tell them now, before they have their secret meeting. Where I know Dana would veto me. At least they'll know I'm interested. 'Cause they might not realize it. I should totally go after what I want. But what if I'm not even on their list, because they know Dana's against me? How pathetic would I feel then? Not to mention I'd be putting Nakili and Miko on the spot, after they've been so nice to me.

CHAPTER FOUR

"Well, uh, bye, see you later." Rockett waved to the CSGs as she made a left, down the corridor to her next class, and they — all three of them — darted into the girls' room.

Rockett had spent nearly the whole art period obsessing about whether to come out and volunteer to be on their ticket. She'd wondered, too, if she should let them know about Nicole's invitation to join *her* ticket. Which could make a difference in their deliberations — if they were even considering her. In the end, though, Rockett wimped out. Shied away from saying *anything*.

That bothered her. As she headed to math, she realized it was all because of Dana. Being afraid of her, that is. But it was too late now. The CSGs were off to their private meeting.

"So *there* you are!"

Lost in chastising herself, Rockett hadn't seen Nicole until she was almost on top of her. Nicole immediately launched into an attack!

"Did I not ask you, like an *eternity* ago, to join our team? Have you even bothered to say *one word about it* since? Not even." Nicole's hand was on her hip, accusingly. Worse, she didn't give Rockett a chance to respond.

"So at first I thought, Rockett's playing hard to get! And then I realized, no, no, Nicole, that's *not* our straightforward little Rockett-girl. She's just too . . . transparent . . . for that. The reason she hasn't answered is that she can't decide — because she needs more information! I'm right, aren't I?"

Nicole's look was classic: Rockett almost wished she could take a picture of it. Then she could put it in the yearbook under: BIGGEST SUPERIORITY COMPLEX.

Wrong, Nicole. The reason I haven't answered you is because I don't trust you — I don't know what's up your designer sleeve. And besides, a little more than a week hardly qualifies as "an eternity." But Rockett didn't say that. Instead, she went, "That's it, Nicole. You're right. I need more information."

Nicole glowed with satisfaction. "I knew it! Here's what I decided. You will sit with us at lunch today. During which time, I will explain our entire platform. Then it will be clear to you, Rockett, that not only is The Ones party the winning party, but we are the deserving ticket. We know what's best for Whistling Pines."

Nicole started to breeze away. With a wave, she added, "See you at lunch. We're at Table . . . One. But then again, the whole school knows where we sit. Even you, as I recall."

That girl is so infuriating! What makes her think every time she snaps her fingers, I'll jump? But . . . she did ask me to be on her ticket — and that is pretty major. It's even possible she has a worthy platform. If I sit with her, at least I'll hear what it is. But, wait, that could be really uncomfortable if Nicole hasn't told Whitney yet. And besides, I promised Jessie I'd sit with her. She has that secret to show us. But I'm sure she'd understand if I told her I needed to sit with The Ones just for today.

In the school cafeteria, Rockett ended up being the first person at the table. In the lunch line, her choices had been franks and beans, or cheeseburgers, or pepperoni pizza. Rockett looked down at her tray and frowned. The salad looked wilted already and the yogurt selection hadn't included any of her favorite flavors. Even dessert, the chocolate pudding, didn't excite her. It was coated with a thick layer of mystery crust. The CSGs had a major point, which she'd realized her first day: The cafeteria food was hurting.

Had she sat with Nicole, she could have found out The Ones' position on that. But this time, Rockett decided not to blow off her friends. Nicole could wait.

Right now, Jessie had a secret to share: and friends are people who share stuff.

Only right now, someone else, neither Jessie nor Darnetta, materialized. Mavis Depew, self-proclaimed psychic, who sometimes sat with them, set her tray down and looked at Rockett hesitantly. Like, *Is it okay if I sit here?*

Rockett shot her a friendly smile. Mavis was, like Arnold, one of the kids who seemed to wear a MOCK ME sign. Which was her own doing. Like she purposely tried to be an outsider. She dressed weird; she acted weird. But so far, Mavis had been nothing but kind to Rockett. And she *was* intriguing. Rockett wondered, "So what's your take on class elections, Mavis? Got a prediction on who'll win?"

Mavis set her tray down and slid in next to Rockett. She scoffed. "You don't have to be psychic to know that. The Ones will win. They always do. No matter what Mr. Baldus says, it *is* a popularity contest."

"But things could change, you never know."

"Unlike you, I do know, Rockett. Take my word for it."

Just then, Jessie blasted over. Her freckled cheeks were flushed as she plopped her tray down on the table and grabbed a section of bench across from Rockett and Mavis. "Hey, guys — sorry I'm late."

Rockett looked around. "Where's Darnetta?"

"Would you believe — she couldn't make it. She's on the audiovisual squad and had to rearrange some science slides that some bozo messed up. I went with her, that's why I'm late."

Rockett assumed that the new lunch equation — minus Darnetta, and plus Mavis — meant that Jessie wasn't going to share the secret. Rockett almost felt bummed that she hadn't sat with Nicole!

But she'd assumed wrong.

For Jessie got right to it. "I'm actually glad you're here, Mavis. Maybe you can help me figure this out."

Mavis lit up. "My psychic powers are at your disposal, Jessie."

A second later, though, Mavis frowned, her nose in

35

the air. For what Jessie produced — a Magic 8 Ball — didn't interest her. "Who needs that? I always know what's going to happen. I don't need artificial devices."

Jessie explained how she got it. "My mom asked me to put a letter in our mailbox, so it would be picked up the next day. I didn't expect there to be anything inside — after all, it was Sunday. But there was this box — a present for me. Attached was a card with my name on it."

Jessie described the note as Rockett examined her gift, a Magic 8 Ball. Supposedly, you asked the ball questions about the future, and answers came on a tiny screen set into it.

Jessie asked Mavis, "All right, maybe you don't need this to predict the future. But can you tell me who gave it to me? It is a guy, right?"

Mavis tented her fingers and pressed her lips together. "You have a secret admirer, Jessica!"

Jessie rolled her eyes. "Gee, thanks, Mavis. I really needed your sixth sense for that! His note said he goes to our school, even. But who is he?"

Mavis got this faraway look in her eyes. "He doesn't want you to know. Yet. But I predict that he will reveal himself." Rockett wondered if Mavis just made this stuff up as she went along.

Suddenly Jessie made a face. "What if it's someone I don't . . . what if it's, like, Arnold or somebody?"

"It isn't." Mavis sounded pretty definite about that. Jessie liked that answer, so she didn't challenge her.

Then Mavis turned to Rockett. "I am feeling some

strong signals coming from you, Rockett. I think you're harboring a secret. And I think you don't want us to know. . . ."

As if on cue — Nicole sashayed over. Well, not exactly over, not like she was headed that way on purpose. Nicole made it look like she was only passing by randomly. But she did stop. To glare at Rockett.

"I see you decided to sit with the . . ." A week ago, she would have said *losers* — or worse — but begrudgingly, she went with, ". . . *them*. Can I wrench you away from your . . . BFs . . . to speak to you, in private?"

Rockett took a deep breath. "I'll be right back," she told Jessie and Mavis.

Jessie tapped her watch. "I promised 'Netta I'd come back to help her, so I gotta leave soon. Don't sweat it, Rockett. We'll see you later."

I hope Jessie doesn't think I'm bailing on her, Rockett thought as she followed Nicole out of the lunchroom.

"What's *with* you, Rockett? Don't you even want to hear about our platform?" Nicole growled the second they were out the door. "If you're turning me down — which would be a huge mistake, by the way — just say it, so I can get on with my campaign!"

Rockett folded her arms defensively. "C'mon, Nicole, give me some space, okay? I haven't made a decision yet. And you're right, I do need to hear what your platform is. But I already told Jessie I'd sit with her — which you didn't give me a chance to explain before. I can't just dump my friends because you snap your fingers."

Nicole rolled her eyes, but let Rockett's words sink in.

Emboldened, Rockett added, "And besides, speaking of dumping your friends . . . have you even told Whitney that she might not be on the ticket? Obviously, she still thinks she is. What kind of friend *are* you, Nicole?"

Nicole grimaced and put her hand up. "Stop! Whitney is not the issue! By the end of today, I will have explained everything to her, and she will totally understand."

"Understand? *I* don't even get it. Why *did* you ask me to be part of your ticket, anyway? It's not like we're friends."

"Well, *chuh*! You're so smart, Rockett, I thought you'd have figured it out. To round out the ticket, of course! If it's just The Ones, it might look . . . oh, I don't know . . . too insular." Nicole let that last word roll off her tongue. "With new blood on the ticket — especially such the indie-girl like you . . . someone unaligned with any clique . . ."

Rockett started to steam. She knew what Nicole meant: someone without any real group to belong to. Yet.

"Anyway," Nicole prattled on, "I know I can't expect you to decide until you know what our issues are. So since you bailed on sitting with us at lunch just meet us in the girls' room after eighth period and we'll go over it. Deal?"

Rockett shook her head. "I told Whitney I'd go home with her right after school so I can help her with language arts homework."

"Handled," Nicole said, too quickly.

"How can it be handled? What are you talking about?"

"By the end of eighth period, I guarantee — not only will Whitney be looped into the entire sitch, she'll even be present at our meeting. You'll have her blessing, Rockett, I promise."

Rockett walked away, unsure of what Nicole was up to. The word *promise*, when used by Nicole, could mean almost anything.

She got a clue later in the day. PE — gym — was her next-to-last period. Rockett had already changed and was out on the gym floor doing the warm-up exercises when she realized she'd forgotten her scrunchie. When she darted back into the locker room to get it, she overheard a convo — definitely not meant for her ears. She felt like an eavesdropper.

It was between Nicole, Stephanie, and Whitney. Nicole's voice was shrill. Stephanie's tense — and Whitney's devastated.

I know exactly what's happening! Nicole's telling Whitney about me! I can't just walk in on them. I better turn around and leave so they don't see me. But maybe it's better if I do sort of innocently appear. That would clear the air for sure. But it might make Whitney feel worse.

Confession Session

How dare Rockett not sit with us at lunch, after I went out of my way to invite her? The little ingrate! Doesn't she realize how important it could be for her standing here at WP to be seen with me? I was right to ask her to join The Ones election ticket. I *must* keep tabs on her and exert influence over her. She's too independent for her own good. And certainly for mine!

I hate Nicole! How could she do this to me? Pushing me off the ticket . . . for Rockett? She doesn't even like Rockett! What's up with that? I wish I could hate Rockett, but . . . I don't. She agreed to help me with the homework. But that's not the only reason I like her — that would be so superficial! Which I'm not!

A fight between my two bests? Why does this always happen? Why am I always in the middle? I hate taking sides, but this time is different. Nicole's got the real — and Whitney's got to realize it. We all have to make some sacrifices for the good of the team.
I wonder what Nicole wants to see Rockett about? I'm feeling so up that I'm totally not insulted that Rockett went with her — obviously, she chose to sit with me instead of her. I'm sure Rockett will tell me all about it.

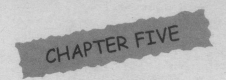

CHAPTER FIVE

Rockett's stomach was twisted in pretzel knots when she slowly opened the girls' room door. It was about fifteen minutes after school had ended. Because she'd decided *not* to barge in on The Ones' fight in the locker room, she didn't know what to expect.

To her relief, all three girls — Nicole, Whitney, and Stephanie — were there. Nicole was clearly pleased that she'd gotten Rockett to show up this time. Stephanie's expression betrayed her anxiety. Whitney just looked trashed.

"Glad you could make it — this time, Rockett," Nicole said with only a trace of a sneer.

Stephanie jumped in, nervously. "Right. Cool. So let's get into the reason we're here. You need to know what The Ones stand for. . . ."

But Rockett stopped her. "Wait — just one minute." What she needed more than that was to hear *Whitney* say something. Anything. Rockett prodded, "Look, Whitney, I just . . . I'm just here to listen. I haven't made any sort of commitment, or even thought about it that much. It's all new to me, a kind of keeping-my-options-open thing. That's all. . . ." she trailed off.

Flatly, Whitney said, "You should accept Nicole's offer."

"Whitney!" scolded Nicole. "Let the girl hear what we stand for first."

"Right." Whitney turned to the mirror over the sink and began applying lip liner.

She wants to make it seem like it's all no big to her, but I know: Whitney feels so betrayed. How could she not? I feel bad for her. But I'm here, so I might as well just listen to what they're saying.

Stephanie and Nicole were explaining something about "quality of life" issues. It seemed to Rockett that they were reading it, speechlike, trading off sentences.

"We, The Ones, know what's best for Whistling Pines," Nicole started. Stephanie picked it up. "We know what you, the students, want. Let's get rid of that stupid rule about no wearing of flip-flops. And those of us who want to carry cell phones should be able to — it's the new millennium!"

Nicole: "We want more dances, since we live in a social world, and it's never too early to learn the art of socializing."

Stephanie: "We definitely want fewer tests and . . . No Homework Fridays!"

Nicole: "The food in the cafeteria must be upgraded — no expense must be spared!"

Stephanie: "And for the class trip, we propose an overnight to Chicago. With *lots* of free time to shop!"

"So, Rockett — pretty amazing platform, right?"

43

Nicole managed to congratulate herself before Rockett could react.

She took her time doing so. The class trip idea was pretty much the only part of their platform that appealed to her — going to the Art Institute of Chicago, that is. Then she said, "Do you really think you have a shot at getting *any* of this — even if you do win? Won't the teachers have something to say, like, 'No way!'"

Nicole scoffed. "*That's* what you think? That we're all empty promises? You know nothing. The Ones are totally powerful, and as the voice of the student body, we can get things done. You can decide to be in the inner circle, or on the outside — looking in. The choice is yours: Vice President Rockett Movado, or . . . Rockett who?"

Nicole and Steph high-fived at Nicole's "clever." Whitney continued to occupy herself at the mirror. "So what's it gonna be, Rockett?" Nicole demanded.

"I need some more time to think about it," Rockett finally said.

"Ticktock, time's running out. We need to declare by the end of the week," Stephanie noted. "Let us know sooner, okay?"

Instead of responding, Rockett walked over to Whitney. "Are we still, you know, on for this afternoon? At your house?"

Without looking at her, Whitney replied, "Sure. Why wouldn't we be?"

*   *   *

Still pretty new in school, Rockett hadn't been to the homes of many Whistling Pines kids. Jessie's, of course, and Miko's, once. And that horrible night of the sleep-over at Nicole's — when The Ones trashed Jessie and the two of them had run out, totally humiliated.

Because Whitney was Nicole's close friend, Rockett sort of expected Whitney's house to be just as imposing. So she was surprised to find the Weiss home more like her own, a modest split-level on a block where every house looked pretty much the same.

Whitney's dad had dropped the girls off, and then gone back to work, promising to bring takeout home for dinner. "You'll stay and join us, Rockett?" Mr. Weiss had offered.

But Rockett didn't think so. She was pretty sure Whitney resented her now that Nicole's offer was out in the open. At that moment, Rockett almost wished she hadn't come here at all. "Thanks," she answered Mr. Weiss politely, "but maybe some other time."

Whitney didn't protest.

I bet she wishes she'd never invited me, Rockett thought glumly. Whitney led Rockett up the stairs to her room and got right to the homework. "So, *The Taming of the Screw* . . . yuck."

"Shrew," Rockett corrected her. "That's how they described totally nasty women back in Shakespeare's day. That's the main character, Katharina."

"Mmm, whatever," Whitney responded absentmindedly. "If we have to do a unit on dead writers, why can't we just do *Romeo and Juliet?*" She said nothing else as she poked around her room, clearing space for them to sit. The floor turned out to be the best option, since Whitney's room was, to put it politely, cluttered.

Stuff was piled everywhere — clothes, backpacks, magazines, CDs, mainly. Seashells lined the shelves of her wall unit; Whitney obviously collected them. The walls and bulletin board were plastered with pictures.

Rockett studied them while Whitney went downstairs to get some snacks. Most were snapshots of Whitney and her friends — Rockett recognized The Ones. It dawned on her that these girls really had a history. There were shots of The Ones at birthday parties and pool parties, playing tennis and horseback riding. Rockett thought it odd that there wasn't one family picture in the room. She was drawn to a framed letter on the wall. It was a commendation from Mrs. Herrera on "excellence in mathematics this semester," addressed to a Barbara Whitney Weiss.

"So that's what Cleve meant," Rockett remarked when Whitney reappeared bearing a bag of pretzels, licorice twists, and iced tea. "Your real first name."

Whitney shrugged. "It's never been this huge secret. I don't like it, so I don't use it. No major big."

Without thinking, Rockett blurted, "What is?"

"What is what?"

"The major big — like problem. I mean — only if you

46

want to tell me. Is it — uh, the grade meltdown thing? Or . . . um . . . you know, the . . . election thing?"

Whitney sighed. "Look, Rockett, I'm okay with you being on the ticket instead of me. . . ."

"But I'm *not* — I mean, I haven't even figured it out yet."

Whitney shrugged. "There's nothing to figure. You go with Nicole, you'll be respected at school, your life will be great. . . ."

Just then, the phone rang. Whitney scrambled for it, and turned her back to take the call. Rockett tried not to listen, but she couldn't help noticing the joy in Whitney's voice. Rockett assumed Whitney was talking to one of her friends, until she squealed, "I *know*, Mommy! I miss you soooo much! And I'm gonna do this, you'll see!" Whitney picked at her split ends nervously as she listened to her mom's end of the conversation.

"I'm sure. Just wait! Give Grandma a kiss for me." When she hung up, she folded her arms across her chest and scowled. "You really want to know the major big in my life right now? Okay, there's, like, so many! But my father currently tops the list."

Carefully, Rockett asked, "You're in a fight with him?"

Whitney regarded Rockett curiously for a moment. "My parents are divorced. You knew that, right?"

Rockett did. But only through the grapevine. Whitney had never confided in her before. "Um, I did sort of hear that. I'm, I guess, sorry."

47

"Don't be. It's just that I don't get to see my mom very much."

"She moved to another city?" Rockett guessed.

"Another country."

Rockett gasped. She couldn't imagine *her* mom being so far away. "Forever?"

"It was supposed to be temporary." All at once, it seemed like the air went out of Whitney and she slid to the floor. Resting her head against the side of her bed, she continued, "My grandmother's real sick and my mom had to go take care of her — in Austria. So we don't really know when she's coming back. And . . ." Whitney started to gather steam now. "My dad makes this offer: I'll pay for a trip for you to go to Austria and see her —"

"That's great!" Rockett interrupted.

"But he throws in this huge IF," Whitney explained. "IF I maintain a 3.0 grade average for the entire semester!"

Rockett shrugged, chewing on a licorice twist. "That shouldn't be so hard — you get good grades, right?"

Whitney whined, "I used to. It's just that I've been real unfocused lately. And my father acts like grades are the only thing I should have on my mind. It's like he refuses to realize that I have a life! My *friends* are my life, not him and my stupid grades! And . . . well, it's so twisted."

So that's it! Whitney invited me here because she needs to up her grade in language arts so she can get that trip her father's dangling in front of her. It has nothing to do with want-

ing to be friends with me. What a user! I should just leave now. I don't like feeling used. But then again, her problem is kind of huge, and I could totally help her. On the other hand, if I leave now, after she told me the truth, she might feel like I abandoned her, and we'd probably never be friends.

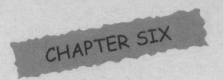

CHAPTER SIX

"Uh, Whitney, you know, this is going to sound so weird, but your problem? It kind of ties in to *The Taming of the Shrew.*"

Whitney threw back her head and laughed. For the first time all afternoon, she seemed lighthearted. "Really? You're funny, Rockett."

Rockett blushed — feeling slightly silly. But it was true. There was at least one parallel between the assignment and what Whitney was going through. The whole thing about your parents not being on your wavelength at all, not understanding what's important to you. Making arbitrary rules that made your life miserable. And over the next two hours, Rockett explained it all. How, in the play, Katharina's sister, Bianca, isn't allowed to get married until Kate does. But Kate is just nasty and has no intention of getting married — ever. The girls even acted out the sections of the play, with Rockett "translating" from the Shakespearean.

When they were done, Whitney looked like this giant weight had been lifted off her shoulders. "Now I totally get it — it's not that hard."

Rockett felt genuinely psyched. It felt awesome to be able to help. She also felt compelled to suggest, "Have you tried telling your dad how you feel? Just talking to him, letting him really understand how much this trip means to you? Maybe if he got it, he wouldn't be so intent on making you keep up a certain average."

Whitney rolled her eyes. "Yeah, like that would work. Forget it."

Rockett let it go, but she did have something else on her mind to ask Whitney about. "There's something else. I need to know how you really feel about me possibly accepting Nicole's offer. Deep truth?"

Whitney suddenly flopped onto her back and stretched out on the carpet. "I'm *okay* with it, Rockett. Really. I mean . . . huge confession: I wasn't at first. I was just so shocked! But after Nicole explained that it would be good for The Ones party to have a balanced ticket . . . well, it does make sense. The main thing is that we win. Everyone already knows I'm a One, so not being on the ticket doesn't really affect my standing at school."

Rockett wasn't convinced — she thought Whitney was totally rationalizing. "Don't you feel even a little betrayed? I mean, the least she could have done was talked to you *before* she asked me, instead of going all stealth on you."

Whitney shrugged. "But then she wouldn't be Nicole. That's not how she operates."

"Then why are you even friends with her?" Rockett could not help herself.

Whitney let out a long sigh and nodded at the pictures that dotted her room. "We've known each other since forever. No one really knows her like I do. She has her problems and deep down . . . well, there's a good person there, Rockett. Really. She's not . . . a shrew!"

They burst out laughing together. Rockett glowed: Whitney got it after all.

"Look, Rockett." Whitney suddenly became serious. "Joining The Ones ticket is a good opportunity for you. It's, like, instant popularity."

Rockett frowned. "But class elections should be about making stuff better, don't you think?"

"That's the cool part, Rockett. First the popular crowd gets elected. Then we make the school better. And okay, Nicole was totally evil to you when you first got here, but she's not the only one on the ticket. Stephanie is really the world's sweetest person. And Cleve — okay, he's a juvie junior-high boy — but he is, like, our star jock and the most popular boy in school. Anyway, don't you want to be popular? It is fun, you know."

Before she could respond, Whitney added thoughtfully, "Everyone talks about popularity like it's this negative thing! But I think it just shows that you're a good, friendly person who people would like to emulate. You sort of *are* that way already, Rockett — Whistling Pines just doesn't know it yet. This could be your chance to let everyone see who you really are."

Whitney's got a point — besides, I really do like her. If I say yes, people will probably see me in a different light — I won't just be the new girl anymore. And just because I say yes to Nicole doesn't make me a snob. I could still be myself,

52

and judge people for who they are inside, not on appearance. On the other hand, except for the school trip suggestion, I don't really agree with The Ones platform. I mean — who cares about flip-flops, cell phones, and more dances? That stuff is so superficial compared to the CSG platform. But reality check — the CSGs haven't asked me. And since Dana has a vote, they probably won't. I should go home and call Nicole and tell her I accept — that would be the best choice.

Which is exactly what Rockett might have done, except the moment she got home, her mom greeted her with a kiss and a message. "Your friend Nakili called. She said it was very important that you call her back right away."

Rockett almost trembled as she punched in Nakili's number: She didn't have long to wonder what was going on. For as soon as Nakili picked up, and then got Miko on three-way, she excitedly got into it.

"The CSG party would formally like to invite you to be part of our ticket — as secretary!"

Oh, no! Being asked by both teams was amazing, maybe even a Whistling Pines first. But it was also majorly scary. Any decision she made was bound to have some icky consequences.

Rockett glowed. "Nakili — that's so cool! Wow! I don't know . . . what to say."

"I suggest 'Yes!'" Nakili shouted.

"Let's tell her who the vice president is," Miko said, a tease in her voice.

"So someone accepted the offer?" It must be the person Nakili was referring to this morning in art class.

"Let her guess," Nakili responded playfully. "I'll give you a clue: It's a boy."

"Oh, thanks — huge clue, Nakili." Rockett laughed. "That only leaves half the eighth-grade population!"

Mischievously, Miko chuckled, "Okay, it's a boy you *know*. And kind of um . . . well, let's say it's a certain boy you sorta like."

Ruben! They were talking about Ruben Rosales? Wow!

"So," Rockett said, stalling for time, "Ruben's on the ticket, huh? It's Nakili for president, Ruben for v.p., Miko for treasurer, and . . ." She trailed off.

"Hopefully you: Rockett Movado for secretary!" Nakili finished.

Suddenly, Rockett *had* to know. "And Dana agreed to this? It was unanimous — all the CSGs voted for me?"

The silence was suddenly deafening. "Eventually," Miko conceded. "It did take some convincing."

Nakili declared, "You're the right person for the ticket, Rockett, and you know it. You're down with everything we stand for. And together, we could create some killer posters and fliers — we are gonna rock this campaign! So what do you say, Rockett? You're with us, right?"

Should I tell them that The Ones asked me? But they might say, 'Oh, forget it, then.' I should be honest and open, right from the start. But I don't even know what I'm doing. I don't want to blow my chances with the CSGs. Or with anybody!

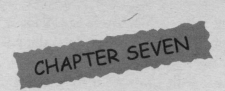

CHAPTER SEVEN

The next morning, Rockett could think about only one thing. *I need to talk to Jessie. In private. I have, like, no time to make this huge decision. I trust Jessie. She can help me.*

But Jessie was not the first person Rockett ran into. Whitney was.

A majorly stressed-out version of Whitney, that is.

"Oh, Rockett, I am so glad I found you! I called your house this morning, but your dad told me you had already left for school. I need you!"

"What's up, Whitney? You've got that discombobulated look down pat," Rockett quipped, to lighten up the moment.

It didn't work. "Look, Rockett, any chance you have that essay you wrote on *The Taming of the Shrew* — the homework assignment you did when your class was on that unit? I need to review it."

Rockett was confused. "But I thought, after yesterday, you got it."

"I thought I did, too. I mean, I did. But now that it's the next day, it doesn't look right to me. Could I just — "

"I'm not exactly sure how seeing mine will help," Rockett said warily, before unbuckling her backpack and retrieving the essay she'd written. Lucky for Whitney, she still had it, since her class wasn't quite done with Shakespeare yet.

"Of course it will! I just want to be sure I covered the important stuff. And don't worry, it's not like I'm gonna copy it or anything. I just think my essay might be kind of off in certain places."

Rockett hesitated.

Whitney whined, "At dinner, my dad got into this huge thing, reminding me that it didn't look like I was going to make the 3.0. He even did this graph on the computer, tracking the grades I've gotten so far in each class — all my quizzes and reports and tests. And now I'm berserko."

Rockett instantly empathized. "Sure. Here you go." She handed Whitney her essay.

"Thanks! You're a lifesaver. I'll get it back to you by lunch."

By lunch? Why can't she just look at it quickly now? We've got time before homeroom. Unless she really is planning on copying it. Maybe I should take it back — tell her I need to fix it or something. But I believe her — I think. She does look majorly stressed out. We're friends. I guess I should just let it go.

"Rockett!" It was Jessie. Her cheeks were all red.

In a flash, Rockett forgot about Whitney and the homework. "Jessie, I so need to talk to you, I was looking for you."

"Here I am — only I can't talk to you now. 'Netta's

waiting in the A/V lab for me. How 'bout we talk at lunch?"

"It's kind of private, Jessie."

"Got it. And Darnetta will be at lunch."

"It's not that I don't like her, it's just that — well, for the moment, could this just be between the two of us?"

Jessie shot Rockett a knowing smile. "Sure. Let's see, what if we get together right after school? Can it wait until then? Wanna meet . . . how about on the soccer field? Practice starts at four or something, so no one will be there much before."

"I'm there — thanks! And, uh, tell Darnetta if she needs any more help with the slides, I could, you know, pitch in."

As Jessie waved good-bye, she said, "No worries, Rockett. 'Netta knows."

There was someone else Rockett wanted to talk to about the whole election thing: She got her chance in homeroom. Ruben was already at his desk when she got there.

"Hey, Ruben, could I ask you a question?"

Ruben regarded Rockett with a gleam in his eye.

He knows, she thought.

She was right.

"Why did I say yes to the CSG ticket, that's what's on your mind, right, new girl?"

Rockett flushed. "It's just that you don't seem like someone who would . . ."

". . . be into junior-high-school politics? You got that right, *chica*!"

"Then why?" Good thing Rockett refused to let herself hope — even a little — that Ruben would say, "I heard *you* might be on the ticket."

Because he didn't.

Instead, Ruben slid to the edge of his seat and stretched his lanky frame all the way out, so that his feet hit the chair in front of him.

"I like to consider myself someone open to new experiences, you know — and I could be down with test-driving this whole election thing. Maybe I get to play some music during the campaign, attract some new listeners to the Rebel Angels sound, you know."

"But what about . . . well, I know you're not a vegetarian, and veggie meals in the caf *is* one of their issues."

Ruben's eyes twinkled and he pointed to himself. "Me carnivore! You're right. But it's like Nakili said, it's not about veggie, it's about choice. Maybe a more intense salad bar, I'm with that. Besides, we can't just let The Ones roll all over everyone all the time. Some Ones maybe could be taken down a peg, you know?"

"Do you think we . . . the CSGs . . . have a shot?" Rockett timidly asked.

"*Sí!* If everyone caves, The Ones win. That's the point — rage against The Ones machine! Wage a campaign. I'm already composing songs."

He's composing songs! All right! How cool is that? And

creating posters and buttons with Nakili and Miko, that would be sweet! And — I just thought of this — Jessie's getting into the flute, and secretly wants to play with some of the kids who have bands. She could be part of the campaign.

Nakili, Dana, and Miko weren't wasting one second getting the CSG campaign off the ground — even if they didn't have a full ticket yet. When Rockett walked into the art room, they'd already started designing posters. She glanced over Miko's shoulder. The slogan was VOTE CSG! WE'RE ABOUT CHOICE, COMPOST — AND COOL!"

Without thinking, Rockett mused, "What about making it C for Choice, S for School Spirit, and then use G for Groundbreaking, as in the idea for the Rollerblade park? That way, you'll make them remember the name of the party and —"

But Rockett was forced to stop midsentence. Dana suddenly hunched over to hide the poster and griped, "Don't show her anything we're working on! She hasn't even bothered to answer us — and maybe I know why!"

Miko sighed. "Don't be like that, Dana. I thought we agreed."

"Chill!" Nakili ordered.

But Dana was on the bus, and not ready to get off. "Three questions: Was it a mistake to invite Rockett? Is she as open as she pretends to be? Does she have another option she hasn't told you about? Jump in anytime, Rockett!"

Rockett's stomach lurched. How did Dana know everything? Did she make a habit of hiding in the girls' room and "accidentally-on-purpose" overhearing everything?

The damage was done. Rockett took a deep breath — and came clean. "Look, guys, Dana's right. I was asked by another ticket, and everything happened so quickly that I haven't had time to, you know, sort it all out. Please don't take back the invitation. Give me, like, a day or two. Okay?"

Miko and Nakili were stunned. Dana smirked and folded her arms across her chest. She didn't *have* to say, "See? I told you so."

But she did anyway.

Quickly, Rockett added, "I probably would have turned Nicole down if I knew you guys were going to ask me. But . . ." *Should I say, "Look, I know Dana hates me, and I figured there's no way you'd ask me." But that's really putting everyone on the spot. Even though it's the truth.*

Nakili didn't let the awkward silence linger. To what must have been Dana's ultimate chagrin, Nakili got it and took Rockett's side. She practically took the words out of Rockett's mouth. To her friends she said, "Look, y'all, Rockett had no way of knowing we were going to ask her — it's not like we tipped her off or anything. Give her a second to breathe — then, whatever she decides, we're down with it."

Impulsively, Rockett gave Nakili a hug. "Thanks." She didn't add, "You are so cool." But she thought it.

*   *   *

Math wasn't exactly Rockett's best subject. But she was better in geometry than algebra, since at least you could draw shapes in that one. Still, answers didn't just come to her, the way they did for other people. Like Miko, and like Dana, who ruled in math. And definitely like Arnold. That's who Rockett sat next to in eighth-grade math class.

If Arnold hadn't made his crush on her so obvious to the world at large, she wouldn't have minded the seating proximity. But just before the start of class today, when he perched on the end of her desk and leaned toward her, Rockett cringed. Her space felt invaded.

Why does he make me feel so uncomfortable? He's really a nice guy. But I can't help it. Sometimes, Arnold just creeps me out. Like the way he's looking at me now — like he's about to ask me something.

Arnold fidgeted with Rockett's notebook. Which annoyed her. But his mind wasn't on today's assignment. And small talk was not something he'd mastered. So he just blurted, "I'm throwing down the gauntlet."

"You're running for student government," Rockett translated, starting to feel queasy.

Arnold grinned. "I've dubbed my ticket the Spork party, after that brilliant invention, a combination of a spoon, fork, and knife, which the cafeteria must employ! Our mission is —"

But Rockett *had* to stop him. "Look, Arnold, don't take this the wrong way, but just don't ask me to be on

61

your ticket. It's nothing personal. It's just that I've already been asked by two other teams."

Behind his thick glasses, Arnold's eyes narrowed. "Have I said anything about asking you? Nay! I was merely about to solicit your opinion. Which I thought I valued. Now I'm not so sure."

Open mouth, insert foot. Rockett felt like a total dunderhead. She backpedaled. "My bad, Arnold, that was *so* conceited. What can I help you with?"

"Forget it." Arnold stalked back to his seat. He would not talk to her for the rest of the period! Rockett even tried to pass him a note, but he stubbornly refused to open it. Which bugged Rockett more than she thought it would. She even goofed up a few easy problems in her notebook because of it.

Whitney wasn't doing any better — just more publicly. For she had the misfortune of being called up to the blackboard to work out a problem. Whitney was clearly in the land of the lost. She started to write this jumble of shapes and numbers — and then quickly erased them. She was chewing the chalk when the teacher, Mrs. Overmeyer, intervened.

"It's clear you didn't do the assignment, Ms. Weiss," the teacher accused. "Take a seat."

Whitney skulked back to her seat, passing Rockett on the way. Her forlorn look made Rockett feel terrible. Especially since math was the subject Whitney had rocked last semester!

The teacher called on Dana. "Ms. St. Clair, perhaps

you could show the class the difference between an isosceles triangle and a trapezoid."

Confidently, Dana got up and with a few swift motions, did the entire problem without hesitating even once. While giving her explanation, Dana said, "An isosceles triangle — *three* equal sides; a trapezoid, four unequal sides — which throws everyone off."

That was so meant for me! How can I even think about going with the CSGs? Nakili and Miko are amazingly cool, but I'm always going to have to deal with Dana. And she's always going to resent me. Why do they even have to be friends with her?

Confession Session

So I copied Rockett's homework — so what? I mean, sometimes you do things you wouldn't ordinarily do. It's like that whole "All's fair in fashion wars," or something. My circumstances are so totally extenuating. Besides, it's not like we're in the same class. And I even switched around some of the sentences. Mrs. Tinydahl won't know the diff, and Rockett will never find out.

I kinda feel bad that I didn't have time for Rockett this morning. But 'Netta asked first, and she needed me. I'll totally make it up to Rockett this afternoon; she'll have my undivided. I'm feeling so amazingly up! I like being needed. And, okay, I like being admired. But I wish I knew by who!

What I told Rockett? That was true. But, okay, I cop to it. Being in the heat of class elections gets me more time near Nic. Not that I'm into her . . . but I could be. Or I could just as easily be into making a fool of her!
I wish Rockett had come out and told us right away that The Ones asked her. It makes me and Nakili look gullible, and it just gives Dana fuel for her fire. But that isn't the way it is. Is it? Now I'm suddenly not so sure! I wish I could be as sure as Nakili when it comes to this stuff.

Okay, that swipe at Rockett in math wasn't too cool. I know I'm going to have to give her a chance — and I will. Just not today. Because mak-ing Rockett confess in front of Nakili and Miko was the right thing to do.
Close call, whew! Be still my wounded pride.

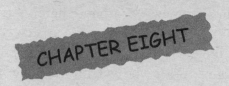
CHAPTER EIGHT

Because Mavis and Darnetta sat with them at lunch, Rockett didn't say anything about the two teams both asking her to join their tickets. It was so *huge* that she had to tell Jessie about it in private. So, instead of blurting out what was really on her mind, she was recounting the events of math class to her lunch buds — until Whitney strolled by.

"You're the best, Rockett — thanks sooo much," Whitney gushed as she handed back *The Taming of the Shrew* essay. "Your homework was an amazing help."

For some reason, Rockett flushed as she mumbled, "No big." She stuffed the assignment into her backpack. But the second Whitney walked away, Jessie was all over Rockett. "What was that about? You let her borrow your homework?"

"Was that . . . a bad thing?"

Darnetta answered, "Not necessarily — if you're sure she didn't copy it."

"Of course she didn't," Rockett scoffed.

Mavis asked. "You know this — for a fact?"

"She said she just needed to look over it to make sure hers wasn't way off base. Come on, you guys, like no one ever compares homework around here? And besides, we're not even in the same language arts class."

"But you have the same teacher," Jessie pointed out. "We don't want to see you get into trouble, that's all."

Why Rockett felt the need to defend Whitney she didn't know, but her words came out more vehemently than she'd intended. "It's just that Whitney's been so stressed lately. And it's not like she doesn't know the work. We went over it. Anyway, is there some deep, dark Whitney secret I don't know?"

Darnetta remarked, "It's not that. It just that she's a One — and from my experience, you can never really trust them. They're users, and they don't care who gets hurt, as long as they get what they want."

At the end of the period, when she and Rockett were returning their trays, Jessie asked, "BTW: What did Nicole want yesterday?"

Rockett whispered, "That's what I have to talk to you about! I can't wait — see you later!"

Only she didn't.

During social studies, Rockett was on the receiving end of two passed notes and on the sending end of another. The class was studying American history. The unit they were on was the Revolutionary War. Mr. Weaseldorf was announcing the details of next week's test when the first note landed on Rockett's desk. It was from Whitney, sitting across the room.

"I don't get this! Why does every single subject have

to be about old stuff and dead people? Why can't we ever do a unit that's circa *now*? I know this is asking a lot, Rockett, but could you puh-leeze study with me? I am so *without* in this class!"

Rockett stared at the note. Whitney was "so without," it was starting to seem, in, like, every class. Okay, exaggeration alert. But this was the third so far that she was obviously struggling in. And the second she'd asked for help in.

I should probably just agree to study with her. But I'm starting to feel uncomfortable. They didn't come out and say it, but obviously Jessie, Darnetta, and Mavis think I shouldn't even be letting her look at my work. I probably should make an excuse why I can't. But then again, it's more than regular grade meltdown — Whitney needs to see her mother. Who wouldn't understand that?

After ten minutes had gone by, Rockett scribbled a note back.

She assumed the next one she got — via Cleve, who was sitting behind her — was Whitney's response. Not even. From the swirly handwriting, Rockett recognized that *this* note was from Nicole.

"We're having a Ones party strategy session after school today. It'll be at the new Let's Get Some 'Za. Which, in case you didn't know, is, like, the hottest place. Be there, or be nowhere."

Rockett was about to answer that one when Mr. Weaseldorf called on her. "Ms. Movado, I know you know the answer to that question." Like Mr. Baldus,

Weaseldorf was usually in a good mood. Genially, he continued, "In fact, that homework assignment you did on Martha Washington showed you have an excellent grasp of the era, and extraordinary insight into it. It would benefit the whole class if you came up and read your essay. Don't forget to show the photos you assembled to illustrate it."

A spotlight-moment was *not* Rockett's favorite thing. But she had no choice. Making the best of it, she trooped up to the front of the room and — swiftly! — gave her report.

Which is why Rockett never got to respond to Nicole's invite. A development Nic was not pleased with. The One, flanked by Whitney and Stephanie, marched up to her desk the split second the bell rang. Nicole's hand was on her hip.

"I know you got my note, Rockett. You'll be there, right?"

"I made some other plans after school, Nicole. So I don't think so."

As if Nicole would give up so easily. "I know what's going on here. You have a trust issue with me, Rockett. But if I weren't totally sincere, why would I let you in on our secret strategy meeting — before you even agree to join us?"

At three-thirty that afternoon, then, Rockett found herself not on the soccer field with Jessie, but sitting in a squishy faux-leather booth at the trendy pizza place, Let's Get Some 'Za, sandwiched between Whitney and Stephanie. Across from her sat Nicole, Cleve, and Max.

70

Although Rockett was incredibly bummed about not getting to talk to Jessie, she'd had her fill of obsessing — she was going to make her choice. Now. At Let's Get Some 'Za!

Jessie had been unexpectedly cool with it. "No big, Rockett. Go with them. Remember, *you're* the one who had to talk to *me*, right? Just don't forget to tell me everything that happens, okay?"

"Every single word," she promised. "In fact, Jess, The Ones, well, that's what I've been wanting to talk to you about. Can I come over to your house tonight? Just for a little while? I'll tell you everything — and believe me, it's a lot!"

Jessie seemed mega-intrigued. "Come right after dinner — do not stop to watch TV!"

"I'll have the number six, the Beverly Hills Pepperoni Pizza, but slice the pepperoni really thin. We're talking *paper* thin! And hold the cheese. And be sure there's no salt. Put the salad dressing on the side. Can you remember all that?"

Nicole was terrorizing the waiter as she rattled off her "custom" personal pie order.

Max elbowed her. "It's pizza, Nicole, not instructions to the troops."

Rockett chuckled. *At least one of them calls her on her bossy ways.*

"Life is in the details, Max," Nicole retorted. "Anyone who's going to help run my campaign should know that."

71

"Yeah, right." Max turned to the waiter. "Make mine the Everything Pie. And do a solid, man? Hold the . . . nothing."

"Make that two," Cleve added. "Plus, supersize sodas all around — it's on Max — his parents' credit card, that is."

"Show-off," Whitney chided him, and kicked him under the table.

Rockett was psyched to see three kinds of veggie pies on the menu and asked for the one with whole-wheat crust.

As soon as the waiter left, Nicole got right to it. Tapping her manicured nails on the table, she leaned back and said, "So, Rockett. What an interesting position you find yourself in — new to the school, and such the wanted one! Not only have I graciously invited you to join our ticket — as vice president, no less — but word is, some random group has also approached you."

Rockett shouldn't have been surprised that Nicole knew about the CSG offer. There wasn't much that Nicole and The Ones didn't find out about. But she was determined to play it cool.

"I haven't made up my mind. Anyway, I thought this was supposed to be a strategy meeting."

"And so it is. But" — Nicole narrowed her eyes at Rockett — "I say we clear the air first. . . ."

"If you really mean that," Rockett interrupted, "how about telling me — with everyone here — why you even invited me to be on your ticket. It's not like we're friends."

Nicole yawned. "How *new*. Come on, Rockett, let it go."

Stephanie tilted her head. "You know, Rockett, you should learn to be a little flexible. Go with the flow. Like Nic says, Ruben note? *Ancient* history."

Max chimed in. "Besides, who hasn't had a little joke played on them every once in a while? If you stayed mad at everyone who dissed you, you wouldn't have any friends. Right?"

Rockett regarded the kids at the table. No matter what anyone said about them, they *were* friends. A fun-loving, carefree bunch who — to be honest — most of the kids at school looked up to and wanted to hang with. That whole thing Whitney said about being popular came back to her. She relaxed. A little.

"Okay, but why me? There are so many other people in your . . . group . . . you could ask. Whitney, for instance."

Rockett thought she felt Whitney tense.

Nicole snapped, "Didn't we already have this convo, Rockett? Like I explained, I believe in diversity. And you bring the indie vote with you. It gives us even more credibility than we already have."

Stephanie weighed in. "Not to mention your artistic talents. We plan on putting a seasonal flower arrangement in every classroom, to beautify Whistling Pines.

73

You could help us with color schemes. Then," she continued, "we heard what a phat photographer you are, which will come in handy for us."

Rockett lit up — she *was* a talented photographer. If she could contribute her ideas and her creativity to the ticket, maybe it *would* be a good idea to go with them.

Excitedly, Nicole's hands flew as she described their campaign poster idea. "We'll pose, the four of us — me in the middle, surrounded by Cleve, Stephanie, and you — with *milk mustaches*! Our slogan will be, 'Got Friends?'"

Rockett's enthusiasm dimmed. Besides being majorly unoriginal, what exactly did that have to do with any issues? Even their superficial ones?

As if reading her mind, Max explained, "See, underneath, in smaller letters, it's gonna say, 'Make The Ones your friends, and we will fight for you.'" He added, "Pretty brilliant, huh? If I do say so myself."

"And I'm supposed . . . to take the picture?" Rockett asked warily.

"Sure," Cleve responded. "You have one of those delayed thingies where you can set it up and then run around and get in the picture? If you don't, Max's dad can get you one. On the house."

"Will you *stop* showing off?" Whitney was at it again — but her tone was far from annoyed.

"I'm not showing off, *Bar*-ba-ra!" Cleve teased. "I'm being practical."

While Rockett was relieved to see Whitney flirting —

instead of hurting — still, something about the whole scene bugged her. She couldn't put her finger on it, until the conversation took an unexpected one-eighty from the campaign.

A girl walked by and Stephanie acted like she'd been tossed by a tsunami. "I! Don't! Believe! It!"

"What?" Nicole asked. Everyone looked up.

Stephanie pointed. "Kirsten just came in? And did you see what she's wearing? The same dress Kristin bought at the Mezzo sale on Saturday."

Nicole's hand flew to her mouth. "Can you imagine if they both wear it. . . ."

Rockett zoned out. She looked over at Max, who was pulling something out of his backpack — a handheld video game. Cleve's eyes lit up. "*Assault* challenge? Whoo-hoo!" He quickly pulled an electronic gadget from his backpack, and the two began a spirited competition.

Suddenly, as if she hadn't realized Rockett wasn't into the fashion chat, Stephanie declared, "Next weekend, Rockett, you are totally coming with us to the mall."

"I am?" Before Rockett could decide if she liked that idea or not, Stephanie did her rendition of tactful — which, unsurprisingly, was anything but. "How do I put this? It's not that your wardrobe needs upgrading, just a little . . ."

"It screams twentieth century," Nicole finished dismissively. "Those little artistic decorations? They are so junior high school!"

"Twentieth century!" Whitney jumped in as if someone had turned a switch on. "That reminds me! The nineties party that Kim had the other week? I forgot to tell you that she told Talia that a certain someone has a crush on someone not in our group!"

"Wait — Talia was there?" Stephanie looked beyond puzzled.

"*Everyone* was there," Nicole noted, not missing a beat.

Except me. What am I doing with them, anyway? They're already trying to change the way I look. Like I'm not good enough for them the way I am. . . . I should just tell them thanks but no thanks, and scoot. But what if that's really dumb? I mean, they seem sincere about wanting me on the ticket — and I am friends with Whitney. And Cleve and Max are kind of fun. And . . . well, it's like the whole school wants to hang with them. But they're asking me.

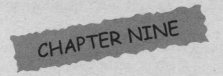

CHAPTER NINE

As promised, that night Rockett went over to Jessie's. Like Whitney's, Jessie's folks were also divorced, but her situation was a little different. For one thing, Jessie lived with her mom, Dr. Swallowfeld. Jessie's older brother, Emilio, was away at college.

Jessie led Rockett into the family room and closed the set of double doors so they could have total privacy.

"Spill all!" Jessie demanded, pretty much the second Rockett sank into the couch.

Rockett took a deep breath. "Things are so weird. Like someone hit the fast-forward button on my life."

Jessie, who'd settled on the hassock across from Rockett, got it. "I'm with you — mine, too!"

Rockett didn't stop to ask Jessie what she meant by that, but launched into the entire sitch. First, the invitation from Nicole to join The Ones party.

Jessie's jaw dropped. "Oh, Rockett — that's what Nicole wanted? That's amazing!"

"But wait, there's more. Then Nakili called — and asked me to join their ticket."

Jessie jumped up from the hassock. "Rockett, that's so . . . wow!" She started to pace the room. "But, okay, the way I see it? It's not much of a choice."

"It isn't? Wait . . . you haven't heard what their issues are."

Jessie stopped short and shrugged. "Doesn't matter."

"Of course it matters, Jessie! What are you saying?"

Jessie took a deep breath and then sat down again on the hassock. She leaned in toward her friend. "Look, Rockett, The Ones are going to win. You should go with them."

Rockett scrunched her nose. "But their issues are so superficial — it's all about stuff they care about. I mean — flip-flops! Come on! What the CSGs want is so real."

"What's that got to do with anything? Once you're on the ticket, you can *change* the platform, add your own ideas. You'll be vice president, after all!"

Rockett paused. She hadn't considered that angle. "You think?"

"And remember, the CSGs only asked you to be secretary. That's not nearly as big a deal. And, let me ask you this — have they even told you what CSG stands for? I mean, if you're going to be on their ticket, they should trust you enough to tell you."

Rockett wavered. "Speaking of not trusting anyone, Nicole and The Ones top that list. You know how evil they can be. Why would you want me to go with them?"

Jessie exhaled hard and her bangs puffed out. "Not all of them are like that. Stephanie asked me to help out with this animal shelter fund-raiser her dad's involved with. So that's pretty cool. And there might be some others I think are okay. . . ."

If Rockett hadn't been deep into her own dilemma,

she might have picked up on Jessie's hint about "some others."

But she didn't. "I feel, I don't know, like me and the CSGs — well, two out of three — are like, just make more sense. Or something."

Jessie tilted her head. "Are you sure that's it? Look, Rockett, I'm your friend so I can say this. Don't make this about Ruben. Don't go with Nakili's team because you have a crush on him."

Rockett got defensive. This time, *she* jumped up. "It's *so* not about Ruben! I just have fun when I'm with them. And, if you want to know the truth, I was thinking about you, too. Ruben's composing music for their campaign, and maybe you could do the flute thing with us. That would be fun. We could all get into it. Darnetta, too." Rockett tossed in that last one impulsively — she wasn't even sure why! Somehow, at that second, it was like she just had to convince Jessie of the worthiness of the CSGs.

Jessie reached up and touched Rockett's shoulder. "I like them, too. And that's so sweet that you're thinking of including me and 'Netta. But the CSGs are gonna lose. And joining them is lose-*lose* for you. You'll make mortal enemies of The Ones, who aren't used to being turned down, and then you won't even have the opportunity to do anything for the school. You'll be nowhere."

Stubbornly, Rockett insisted, "I'm sorry, Jess. I can't agree. It's only a given that The Ones will win if everyone just assumes so, and caves."

Suddenly, Jessie grinned. "I have an idea. Let's see what my Magic 8 Ball says." She ran off to her bedroom to get it. When she returned, she handed it to Rockett. "Here. You ask it."

Feeling a little silly still, Rockett did. Cupping the ball in both hands and rotating it, she whispered, "Tell me, Magic 8 Ball, will The Ones party win the election at Whistling Pines Junior High?"

The answer came up quickly. And absolutely. YES.

When Rockett got home that night, there were two messages for her.

Whitney wanted to talk about the note Rockett had passed her in social studies. It had said, "I totally want to help, Whitney, but I'm not that great in every single subject. How about asking Nicole or Steph?"

Now Whitney whined, "I *can't* ask them. They don't even know about the whole trip my father's blackmailing me with!"

"Are you embarrassed to tell them?" Rockett guessed.

"My own friends? Not! It's just that, you don't know her all that well, but Nicole has her own stuff to deal with. Serious stuff, Rockett — and please don't ask me to explain. I can't."

Serious stuff, huh? Like deciding if wearing one designer's outfit with another designer's shoes is mixing genres or something? Wait, that's mean. I better not say that.

"Well, what about Stephanie?" Rockett tried again.

"You said she's the sweetest person. I bet she'd be willing to help."

Whitney sighed. "Steph is the greatest, but she's no brain surgeon. Come on, Rockett, please, you know why this is so critical. I have to do well this marking period, or I don't get the trip to see my mom."

Rockett crumbled. "Okay, but just for this marking period, social studies, math, and language arts."

Then Rockett returned Nakili's call. Her friend was bubbling with excitement. "I know you didn't decide, and I'm not trying to sway you, but you gotta listen to this!" Then, she put on a tape of the campaign song Ruben was working on. It went something like, "Rock 'n Rollerblading, recycling, and relating, adjust your 'tude, bust a move, the CSGs will rock the school!"

The hooky rhyme stayed in Rockett's head all night.

The next day, Rockett had a hard time staying focused. She was totally off in space, obsessing about her decision. And rationalizing.

I want to go with the CSGs, but Jessie's right. I should go with The Ones. It's win-win. They'll win, and I'll get them to accept some of my ideas. I'll still be myself, but I'll just hang with them sometimes. Miko and Nakili will understand. They could easily get someone else on the ticket. I mean, now that Ruben's on, I bet some people he's tight with, like Arrow or Viva or Ginger, would go with them.

After language arts, she was going to collar Nicole and tell her she'd accepted. Whew! Finally — that weight would be off her shoulders! Rockett should have felt majorly relieved as she slipped into her seat in Mrs. Tinydahl's class. The class was still on the last part of its Shakespeare unit. The discussion was on *Hamlet* and today's lesson centered on one of the most famous lines in that play. Mrs. Tinydahl had written it on the blackboard.

THIS ABOVE ALL, TO THINE OWN SELF BE TRUE.

The teacher faced her class. "Put your books away," she instructed. "I want to talk about this quote. I want to know what it means — not to Hamlet, but to you. Does it have any relevance in your own life? Who would like to start?"

Rhetorical-question alert. As usual, Mrs. Tinydahl didn't wait for volunteers. She called on Max. "Mr. Diamond? What does that quote mean to you?"

Flustered, Max frantically paged through his copy of the play. "Uh, what scene was that one in?"

Mrs. Tinydahl frowned. "You didn't hear me — I said, put the books away. I want to know what the quote means. To you, in your own life."

Max went into cover-up mode, picking up steam as he went along. "Uh, that one's really deep. It requires far more time to explain than one single period of eighth-grade English. I mean, *c'mon*, Mrs. T! You know what I'm sayin'?"

"I do know, Mr. *D*. It means you have no clue." Be-

82

fore Max could protest, Mrs. Tinydahl turned to single out her next victim. A broad smile lit up her face when she realized someone had actually raised her hand.

"Stephanie? You have a take on this?"

"Does this Shakespeare stuff satisfy the foreign language requirement?"

Mrs. Tinydahl groaned. "No, Ms. Hollis, it doesn't."

Another hand shot up. "Dana?" Mrs. Tinydahl said, this time a little less hopefully.

Dana went for it. "It means know who you are and what you want. And then go after it — no matter who might be trying to stop you."

Was it Rockett's imagination, or did Dana totally shoot her an accusing look?

Dana had opened the door — soon, the rest of the class was, as Ruben wittily put it, "gettin' bardy wit' it."

Cleve's interpretation was, "Hey, if you've got it, flaunt it!"

Chaz, who was tight with Cleve and Max, added his interpretation: "No wimps! It means my way or the highway."

For the first time Rockett could recall, that goth-girl, Sharla Norvell, participated — without being called on. Her take? "It's bull."

Mrs. Tinydahl was shocked. And intrigued. "In what way is it . . . bull, Ms. Norvell?"

Sharla rolled her eyes. "Be true to yourself — yeah, right. As long as you conform. The minute you're different, wham! No one wants to be around you. Typical."

"Who agrees with Sharla?" Mrs. Tinydahl ventured.

If there'd been a picture balloon atop Rockett's head, you would have seen Mavis and Arnold in it. But they weren't in this class, so they couldn't agree. Instead, it was Wolf who raised his hand. "It's not that I agree. But I *hear* her. The way I see it, it's a spiritual thing. Follow your spirit guide, even if it takes you away from the pack."

Without waiting to be recognized, Nicole announced, "I agree with Wolf."

Rockett's jaw dropped. She does? Nicole must have a major jones for Wolf — her whole life is the *opposite* of what Wolf just said. Does she think he'd be so flattered not to recognize her hypocrisy? But no one challenged Nicole, and if Wolf noticed, he didn't let on.

Nakili was called on next. "It means don't follow the crowd. Do what your *heart* or your spirit guide, or whatever you want to call it, tells you. Even if it makes you unpopular."

In the end, Rockett responded. She surprised herself when she said, "It means you don't always have to be who others want you to be."

Just before the bell rang, Mrs. Tinydahl gave the assignment for tomorrow. She added, "Ms. Movado — please see me before you leave."

As her classmates filed through the door, Rockett made her way up to the teacher's desk. She assumed Mrs.

84

T was going to compliment her on her excellent interpretation of the quote.

Which is why Rockett felt like she'd taken a stab to the abs when her teacher said, "*The Taming of the Shrew* — our class is done with it. But my other class is on that play. As I'm sure you know, Whitney Weiss is in that class."

Rockett stood there, unsure of what was coming — but just sure enough to dread it. Mrs. T continued, "Whitney's been struggling lately. And I'm not going to beat around the bush, Rockett. The homework she turned in looked suspiciously like yours. I'll show you what I mean." Mrs. Tinydahl had a copy of Rockett's report. She put it next to Whitney's. They weren't exactly the same. Just really close.

"Is there anything you want to tell me?" Mrs. T asked.

I should tell her the truth — I lent it to Whitney and obviously she copied it. But how could I do that? What kind of friend tattles on you — especially when you're having major problems? Whitney would feel so betrayed! But . . . Whitney lied! She told me she wasn't going to copy it. What kind of friend does that make her? I should make sure I don't get in trouble over this.

Confession Session

I got this note from my secret admirer. He said, "I hope Rockett joins The Ones ticket. That could bring you and me closer!" But that's not why I told Rockett to go with them. What I told her is true. The Ones will win, and this is her way to make a difference in the school. So anyway, my secret admirer is obviously a One — or a friend of The Ones. Chaz? Cleve? Max? Wish I knew!

This should have been so easy! Why is Rockett holding out? I want her on the ticket because she could be a powerful influence. People seem to like her. I mean, Whitney's acting like they're best friends or something! What's that about? And Cleve's flirting. If she gets on another ticket, I could . . . lose. Which is so *not* an option.
I think she's getting the message!

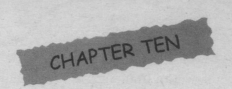

CHAPTER TEN

"Rockett? Did you hear me?" Mrs. Tinydahl was looking at her with something that bordered on annoyance. For Rockett, rooted to the floor, was struck speechless when confronted with the two assignments.

And now she was really on the spot.

"We studied together, Mrs. T," Rockett sputtered. "We acted out the play. It's probably just a coincidence that the homework is so similar."

Mrs. Tinydahl crossed her arms, unconvinced. "I'll let it go, Rockett, but covering for a friend does neither of you any good. And I have to tell you that it's my duty to report this 'coincidence' to Mrs. Herrera."

Rockett turned ashen. Mrs. T softened. "As long as nothing of this nature happens again, it won't go on your permanent record. And knowing you, I'm sure it won't."

Rockett thanked Mrs. Tinydahl and raced to her lockers — desperate to find Whitney. Instead, she found a message from the CSGs, delivered via magnetic letters on her locker door. DID YOU MAKE UP YOUR MIND? DON'T LEAVE US IN A BIND! IN THE ART CLASSROOM, PAINTING POSTERS, IS WHERE THE CSGS YOU'LL FIND!"

Rockett snatched the letters off her locker and put

them on Whitney's — rearranged to spell out, HOW COULD YOU DO THIS? YOU KNOW WHAT I MEAN! CALL ME!!

But Whitney didn't. And every time Rockett tried to call her, the line was busy. When she finally did get through, Mr. Weiss informed her that Whitney had spent too much time on the phone tonight already, and not enough on her homework. Unless it was an emergency, it would just have to wait until tomorrow. He added, not unkindly, "You can E-mail her, but she won't read it until the morning, because I've confiscated her computer for the night."

Then, the weirdest thing happened. While tossing and turning in bed, Rockett heard this voice in her head. Mrs. Tinydahl's? *To thine own self be true. What does that mean to you? In your own life?*

And all at once, Rockett had the answer to that.

And she knew exactly what she had to do.

She bolted up, turned on her computer, and typed out an E-mail message. It was only when she pressed SEND that she was able to fall asleep.

The next morning she showed up at Whitney's door, determined to catch her before she left for school.

Whitney was shocked to see Rockett at her door.

"It's the crack of dawn, Rockett. What are you doing here? And, footnote: You look like you hardly slept. I mean, bed-head alert."

89

Rockett had run a quick brush through her hair before getting her mom to drive her to Whitney's, well before school. And Whitney got one thing right. She had barely slept the night before. The events of that afternoon had her totally wiggin'.

"I think you know what I'm doing here, Whitney. I put that note on your locker, telling you to call me, but you didn't and . . ."

Whitney's eyes went wide. "That was *you*? Come on, Rockett — you didn't sign it, how was I to know? I called everyone I could think of."

Oops. So that's why her phone was busy.

"So what's the big emergency?" Whitney asked, leading Rockett upstairs to her room, so she could finish putting on her makeup.

Rockett took a deep breath and closed the door to make sure Mr. Weiss didn't overhear them. "Whitney, did you copy my essay? Mrs. Tinydahl called me up and practically accused me of letting you cheat!"

Whitney stared into her reflection in the mirror and applied her lip liner. Blotting, she replied, "I'd never do that."

Rockett crossed her arms and tapped her foot impatiently. "She *showed* me the two essays, side by side! They were . . ."

Whitney whirled around, now on the offense. "Identical?"

"Not exactly, but . . ."

"But what, then? I mean, it's the same stupid play. I'm

sure half the class had similar essays. How many different things are there to say about it?"

"Enough, I guess, so that of all the papers in both classes, yours and mine won the twin award. And . . . she's reporting it to Mrs. Herrera. It could go on our permanent records!"

Whitney burst out laughing. "Relax, Rockett! First of all, she's bluffing. Second of all, she has no proof — unless you said something? But you couldn't have, because . . . repeat after me, no actual copying occurred. This is bogus. You believe me, don't you?"

Because Mr. Weiss drove them to school, Rockett didn't get a chance to say anything further about the essay. Nor did she get to tell Whitney the second thing she'd come to say.

That didn't happen until they got to school. They'd barely emerged from the car when Nicole was upon them. The One seemed pleased to see them together. "Solidarity! That's what I like to see. You two are carpooling now? Well, this can only mean one thing: Rockett's wised up and decided to join us. Excellent idea."

"You've got one part right, Nicole," Rockett calmly explained. "I did make a decision. But you blew it in the bonus round. . . ." She paused and regarded Whitney, and then looked straight into Nicole's narrowed eyes. "Before I went to sleep, I E-mailed Nakili and told her that I'll be on *her* ticket. Assuming she still wants me."

Whitney gasped.

As for Nicole, there was, like, steam coming out of her ears. "Bad choice," she hissed. "You'll regret it."

Ticked, Rockett challenged, "Is that a threat, Nicole?"

"A threat? I wouldn't call it a mere threat. It's worse. It's a look into the future. Ask your good friend Mavis Depew if you don't believe me. I offered you a golden opportunity, and you blew me off."

With that, Nicole stalked away. Whitney flew after her.

The grapevine is a powerful thing, Rockett learned. By the time she got to homeroom, it seemed the entire school knew about her decision. Nakili rushed up and threw her arms around her. "Welcome to the par-*tay*, Rockett! Girl, this is so fly, but I knew you'd make the right choice. I went right to Mrs. Herrera's office and officially signed us all up. We are the CSG party."

Just as Miko said that, it struck Rockett — she was now officially on the CSG ticket, but she still didn't even know what those initials stood for. *How weird is that? I could ask . . . but somehow, the timing doesn't feel right. Everyone's so happy right now. What if asking them was this huge downer? I should probably wait.*

Miko, smiling broadly, handed Rockett a piece of paper with a list on it. "As soon as I heard, I made a list of stuff we're working on, so you could catch up, see where we are. We have so much to do!"

"Starting with," Nakili described, "right after eighth

92

period, come to the art room. We'll show you what we've got done so far and have a brainstorming session."

Nakili and Miko weren't alone. Dana was standing right behind them. To Rockett's mega-surprise, she stepped forward and extended her hand. "Now that you're onboard, we *are* going to work together. We take this seriously, and we want to win. So, you know, welcome."

Zoom — Rockett got it: That was probably so hard for Dana to say. She quickly responded, "Thanks, Dana, I appreciate that. And I . . ."

But with a wave and a nod, Dana walked off and took her seat. Rockett sighed and started down the row to her own seat. Before she got there, someone tapped her on the shoulder.

Ruben. He held up his palm. "Slap me five, new girl! Word is, you're with us. *Muy excelente.* 'Cause it's gonna be uphill."

Rockett hoped he didn't see her blush. "You think so?"

"*Sí.* Anyway, now that you're on the ticket, we're ready to roll."

Rockett glowed. She wanted the moment to last, but the timing was off. The class was filing in, more quickly now. And her "up" bubble was about to be pricked. Cleve and Max brushed by. Their expressions were downright stony. "So, Rockett," Cleve said, stopping, "I hear you won't be needing a new camera, after all. I hope you know what you're doing."

Rockett was determined to be friendly. "It was a tough choice, Cleve, really. I'm flattered that you guys even asked me. So no hard feelings, okay?"

Cleve didn't answer, just shook his head glumly. Rockett turned to Max, who'd remained uncharacteristically silent. Mopey, almost. "You're not mad at me, are you, Max?"

No answer.

She tried again. "I'm sorry if my decision disappointed you, but . . ."

Finally, he grumbled, "Thanks, Rockett. For nothing."

Rockett walked to her seat. *Every choice you make is bound to make some people unhappy. I should have expected The Ones to be majorly annoyed.*

What she didn't expect was someone else — someone whose feelings she'd accidentally hurt — to be irritated at her, too. Jessie was standing by Rockett's desk, arms folded. "So, I guess you decided," she said curtly.

Rockett got flustered. Because she'd been so obsessed with Whitney, and finally figuring out her decision, she'd totally forgotten to loop Jessie in *before* the news got out. "Jess! I am so sorry! But so much happened — I'll tell you all about it — and I just didn't get to call you. My bad."

Jessie couldn't hide her double dose of disappointment. "Sure, Rockett. Whatever. You had more important people to tell first, I guess."

"No, Jessie! It's not like that. It's this whole . . ." She lowered her voice to a whisper. "This thing with Whitney and the language arts homework threw me, and I . . ."

Jessie held up her hand as Mr. Baldus started tapping on the blackboard, a signal for everyone to be seated. "Forget it. We'll talk about it later."

By the time Mr. Baldus blared, "Groovy guys 'n gals of grade eight homeroom, heads up, here comes attendance," Jessie was already in her seat. Rockett had no choice but to scribble a note. *I'm sorry I forgot to tell you, but I think I made the right choice. It felt right, anyway. I hope it's okay with you.*

The one Jessie wrote back betrayed her hurt. *Okay with me? It wasn't my decision. You asked me for advice and didn't take it. Whatever. I totally respect you for following your heart, even if I think your heart's leading you the wrong way. Does that make any sense?*

As Rockett crumpled the note, she was beginning to wonder if anything made any sense. She'd been so self-absorbed, she'd hurt her friend — and for some bizarre reason, Max, too! He was acting more bruised than annoyed — she'd gotten on Nicole's bad side, and she had no clue what Whitney was feeling right now. Was being "true" to yourself worth it?

After Mr. Baldus finished with attendance, he announced, "Let's get to the headline news of the day! I mean the ultra-cool, may-the-best-team-win Whistling Pines election! Mrs. Herrera tells me the teams have all

95

declared. So, for your edification — heh-heh, put that one in your Webster and look it up! — I will now announce the parties officially running for class office."

He read from a printout. "Behind door number one, we have The Ones party. That's Nicole Whittaker, Whitney Weiss, Stephanie Hollis, and Cleveland Goodstaff."

Mr. Baldus had to pause to remind The Ones that they hadn't *won*, and there was no reason to stand up, expecting applause.

"Next on the list is the CSG party. Which consists of Nakili Abuto, Ruben Rosales, Rockett Movado, and Miko Kajiyama.

"And last, but never-ever least, we have the Spork party, Arnold Zeitbaum and Bo Pezanski. Who assure us that between those two able-bodied men, they can handle all four jobs."

Arnold was wearing a campaign button. SPORK POWER! Rockett shot him a friendly thumbs-up but Arnold didn't return the gesture.

Mr. Baldus then declared, "Let the campaigns begin! You have two weeks. After which, in the great spirit of democracy, we'll have a debate. And then, the voting will commence! So let's rock 'n roll!!"

Later, Rockett bumped into Whitney on the lunch line. Rockett had pizza on her tray — she'd already started to peel off the pepperoni slices. On Whitney's was a spectacularly unappealing melange of wilted salad and mystery meat. "Improvements severely required," Rockett pointed out.

"Agreed." Whitney stuck out her tongue. "I can't believe these were our only choices today."

Because Rockett was wary about divulging the CSG platform, she didn't say, "Things will be different when we win." But she wanted to.

There was a moment of awkwardness before they headed to their separate tables. Then, Whitney grasped Rockett's elbow. "I've been thinking about the whole language arts essay trauma-rama. I'm going up to Mrs. Tinydahl to tell her that *you* totally did nothing wrong. And if subconsciously I did make my paper too similar to yours, well, I'm sorry. Don't worry, Rockett, you're in the clear."

Whitney made good on her promise. She showed up at the end of Rockett's language arts period and approached the teacher.

Rockett waited just outside the door. Whitney emerged after a few minutes. As they walked to the lockers together, Whitney assured Rockett that Mrs. T totally understood. No one was actually being accused of cheating.

Rockett confessed, "I'm really glad you did that. I feel better about the whole thing now."

Whitney grinned. "Okay, if we're doing confessions, here's mine to you: I wasn't *ever* really okay with Nicole asking you instead of me to be on the ticket. Anyway, now that you're not, it feels kinda kickin' to be vice president."

"Don't you mean, *running* for vice president?" Rockett reminded her — a little less playfully than she might have.

Whitney giggled. "Sure. Keep hope alive, Rockett."

"So, I guess you're not mad at me the way Nicole, Cleve, and Max are?"

"No way. We're still friends, regardless of this other stuff. I mean, I think you're a cool person. And I'm not like some sheep who just follows Nicole around, you know?"

"I do, Whitney. I really do know that."

"But . . . this does bring up that other tiny prob," Whitney mentioned, just as they reached their lockers. "Now that I have election stuff to deal with, I have, like, even less time to study. Could the timing of the election be any more heinous? This is the same semester I *need* that 3.0."

Rockett tensed — she knew what was coming.

She was right. Whitney lamented, "I know you promised to help me with LA, math, and social studies, and that's so amazing. But . . . I so hate to ask . . . I'm not getting science, either."

Rockett's blood pressure zoomed skyward. She was starting to feel used. "Wait . . ."

"My entire life will be ruined if my grades slip!" Whitney whined. "I have to get that trip! I have to see my mom!"

Suddenly, Rockett had a bolt of inspiration. "What about Arnold? I mean, when it comes to science, *he's* the class brainiac."

"I can't."

"Don't tell me you can't be seen with him or some stupid Nicole-esque reason," Rockett challenged. "Like you just said, you have a mind of your own."

Whitney flushed. "I do, but it's just Arnold. See, he used to have this crush on me, and I wouldn't want him to misinterpret. . . ."

"It's not just about him, right? It's like if anyone saw you guys being study buddies, they might think it was more than that?" Rockett guessed.

If Whitney was going to respond, she didn't get the chance. Just then, Miko strolled by. "Hey, Rockett! No consorting with the enemy! We're meeting in the art room now — come on!"

"I'm there," Rockett responded happily. She was just about to dash off after Miko, glad for an excuse to get away from Whitney, but Whitney got the last word in. "You'll help me, right, Rockett? I mean, just study with me, that's all! We're friends, don't forget, and I need you!"

Confession Session

If I were a different
person, I could really be mad
at Rockett. I mean, she could
have told me first — before the rest of the
school — what she decided. First she asks my
advice, then she not only doesn't take it —
she leaves me out of the whole thing! What
kind of friend does that? All I know is, I
wouldn't. And neither
would 'Netta.

CHAPTER ELEVEN

If Rockett felt like her life was in fast-forward mode before, now it was zooming by at warp speed. But it was all good, extra-crunchy even. For the next two weeks, she spent every spare moment working alongside her teammates. Together, they dreamed up slogans and designed posters to illustrate: YOU, ME, AND THE CSGS — TOGETHER, WE'LL MAKE WP THE PLACE TO BE. To illustrate their veggie platform, Rockett had taken pictures of the selections in the cafeteria every day. Then she made a collage and pasted the menus from other schools around it. WHISTLING PINES NEEDS CHOICES, she'd written.

Miko made sure they had regularly scheduled brainstorming sessions.

"I noticed Arnold's team has campaign buttons," Rockett remarked at the first one. "I came up with a couple of designs for ours — if we agree to have them, anyway."

Nakili nodded. "Buttons are a no-brainer. Let's see whatcha got, Rockett." Rockett produced a series of drawings, which she'd come up with during her afternoon classes. Her favorite featured Rollerblades and said, ZOOM ON OVER TO THE WINNING SIDE!

Dana scribbled on her notepad and held it up. "What

103

about this?" Her design featured the word *Ones* with a diagonal line through it, as in "No Ones."

"Cute," Miko giggled, "but we're not going there."

Ruben vigorously agreed. "I'm not onboard with 'Stamp out The Ones.' We gotta stay positive."

Dana teased, "You're not saying that because of your crush on a certain someOne, are you, Ruben?"

In a flash, Nakili and Miko were in Dana's face. "Don't! We're a team. Let's act like one."

Rockett tried to ignore the sting. Ruben had a crush on Nicole? News bulletin! And, in spite of Dana's pledge for solidarity, Rockett couldn't help wondering if it had been said for her benefit.

In the end, they voted for the Rollerblade design for their official campaign buttons, and Ruben said he'd handle getting them made up. "I got a few more verses down for our campaign song," Ruben said. "Wanna hear?"

As he started to play and sing, Rockett totally tingled. When he was done, they all clapped and cheered. "Can I make a suggestion?" Rockett asked when the applause ceased.

"Suggest away, new girl," Ruben said, putting down his guitar.

"Well, you know Jessie? She plays the flute — she's really good. And I was wondering, would it be okay if she played with us? I know she's not on the ticket or anything . . ."

Nakili gave a thumbs-up. "Why not? The girl's a CSG supporter. She wants to? Let her play."

Rockett heaved a sigh of relief. She didn't know if Jessie even wanted to have anything to do with her, let alone align herself with the CSGs. Mainly, she was just happy to be able to make the offer — without having to point out that Dana wasn't technically on the ticket, either.

Sometimes Rockett thought Jessie was the most forgiving person she'd ever met. Which sometimes made her feel not worthy of Jessie's friendship. She felt mostly grateful, then, when Jessie was all for her suggestion.

"Sure, I'll play the flute with Ruben. That would be fun. After all, I am voting for your team."

"Thanks for not holding a grudge, Jessie."

"What kind of friend holds a grudge? Not me."

Jessie even joined the team when they got to school early the next day to put up posters. The Ones had beaten them to that particular punch already, with their milk mustache posters. Only — uh-oh! — someone had beaten The Ones at their own game. Underneath their GOT FRIENDS? slogan, a joker had scrawled, THESE ARE NOT YOURS!

That seemed to be a signal that the war was on. Later, over Arnold's SPORKS MAKE SENSE, someone had written, ONLY ON PLANET ZITBOMB!

And the next day, someone had defaced their poster as well. Scrawled over ROLL WITH THE CSGS, some joker had crayoned in LOSERS!

The pranks had forced Mrs. Herrera to issue a stern warning, which came over the PA system that very day: "The defacing of campaign posters must cease at once! Or elections will not be held at all!"

That worked.

For about a second.

Between classes, Rockett handed out flyers describing her team's platform. Even while it was discouraging to see some kids crumple them up and toss them like paper airplanes, still Rockett felt completely upbeat. She knew why, too. For the first time since arriving at Whistling Pines, she was really part of something. And it showed: She radiated like a glowworm.

But if anything nicked her mood, it was keeping her promise to Whitney. That girl just seemed to amp up the whining at every study date. She'd go, "We only have a few minutes, I have to go meet Nic and the guys! Let's skim through this, okay?"

"But how are you going to learn, then?" Rockett would remind her. "That's the whole idea."

"You know it's just for now. Do you always have to play by the same exact rules every time, even under extenuating circumstances? Be flexible!"

For the most part, Rockett was. Until the day Whitney, out of impatience with a math problem she couldn't — or wouldn't — focus on, demanded, "Can't you just *show* me the answer?"

Rockett snapped the book shut. "No, Whitney. I better go."

In a flash, Whitney shifted into reverse. "My bad. I didn't mean that exactly. I'm just so stressing. When the election is over, I'll do this myself. I'll get it together. But until then, you of all people should understand!"

Rockett did. She was squeezing in so much, she barely had time to do her own studying. Which is why, when Mr. Weaseldorf hit the class with a surprise announcement, Rockett panicked.

"Because you guys are rocking our unit on the evolution of the Revolution, I've decided to move up the test. Why wait until next week when you all seem to be ready now? What say we take it tomorrow?"

Over the gasps of the class, he added, "Getting ahead of ourselves gives us extra time to use for our next unit, the War of 1812, and it also gives us a free period for a party Friday. Maybe we'll have a small multinational celebration — everyone brings some chow."

A party during social studies? Rockett's class was there. The objections suddenly faded.

Rockett was one of two people severely unthrilled with the date change: Whitney was the other.

But this time, there was little either could do about it. The campaigns were firing up and as Dana reminded one and all, "If you're not one hundred and ten percent with us, you're against us."

That The Ones were two hundred and ten percent against Rockett was something they seemed to take every opportunity to prove. Max frowned every time he passed her in the hallway; Cleve hadn't even made eye contact in, like, a week. In PE, Nicole slammed a dodgeball right at Rockett's shins. Of course, she pretended it was an accident. Yeah, accidentally-on-purpose.

Nakili tried to convince Rockett to keep it in perspective. "It'll all be over and forgotten soon, relax."

"But I'll always have the pictures to remind me," Rockett noted. Wearing her yearbook editor cap, Rockett had decided to snap pictures of the campaign in full swing. She photographed one of Ruben's jam sessions. And she took an entire roll of film of Arnold manning his "election headquarters" booth, next to which he'd erected a giant Spork.

In spite of her partisan position, Rockett totally grooved on capturing the spirit of the election.

Until, that is, The Ones stepped it up. During the second week of the campaign, they came to school each day bearing gifts for their "constituents." One day, it was long-stemmed roses, which they gave out in the hallways, with a slogan A ROSE BY ANY OTHER NAME WOULD BE THE ONES. The next, it was beanbag dolls, with ribbons around them that said THE ONES CARE.

Dana was the first to go ballistic at their new tactic. "Unfair! They're buying votes! I'm going to Mrs. Herrera."

"Go to the Supreme Court for all I care, all's fair in love and war," Stephanie had reminded her, a little too sweetly. "There's no rule against showing the school population that we, The Ones, are with the times. We love Beanie Dolls. Don't you?"

Dana had stormed off in a huff. This time Rockett, just as ticked, had linked arms and joined her. The next day, Dana brought lollipops — to hand out to the students. She'd put a little "CSG" ribbon around each one.

During their last strategy session, Miko handed out papers, divided into three columns. Under the first column, she'd listed the votes they could count on. In the second column were the votes they'd never get. It was the names in the third column Miko was most interested in, the undecideds. "Those are the ones we have to get on our side," she instructed.

In that column, she'd written, "Arrow, Viva, Ginger, Sharla, Wolf, and Mavis."

Ruben leaned back and strummed his guitar. "I'll talk to Arrow, Viva, and Ginger. They're not into the whole political bag, but maybe this time they'll vote. Our way. And Wolf's my man. I'll deal with him."

Nakili grinned. "That's the spirit. Now, Rockett, I was hoping you'd convince Mavis."

Rockett shrugged. "She's got a mind of her own, but I'll try. And . . ."

"What?"

"I might try talking to Sharla, if you think that's a good idea."

"She's a real head case, Rockett," Miko advised. "I don't hold out much hope for her voting at all. I wouldn't waste my time."

Ruben came to Rockett's defense. "I say go for it, new

109

girl. You never know what someone's really thinking, or hiding, unless you reach out. What could happen?"

What happened was this: During the middle of the second week of campaigning, the loyalties of Whistling Pines' students seemed to splinter and split as Rockett's classmates began declaring who they'd vote for. And a funny thing happened along the way: The Ones' assumption of a landslide? It was all, "Not so fast."

For the CSGs proved a stronger draw than most people — especially The Ones — would have imagined. Especially after Ruben gave impromptu Rock the Vote concerts in the hallway during lunch hour; Jessie joined him on flute as Rockett, Miko, Nakili, and Dana stood nearby handing out flyers and buttons.

The first time, Cleve and Max tried to heckle Ruben, making up phony words to the songs, but even before the teachers could discipline them, they were shushed by the kids grooving to Ruben's beat.

"Good sign for us!" Miko had declared gaily.

The Ones "retaliated" by hiring a professional deejay and hosting a Flip-flop Freedom Vote bash on the soccer field after school. It seemed like the whole student body was there!

"Bad sign for us." Miko flip-flopped her calculation.

The Sporks stayed the course, as Arnold called it. "We couldn't lower ourselves to that. We answer to a higher power." Everyone knew that neither he nor his running mate — who basically hadn't done anything to help, so far as Rockett could tell — could compete with the contest the other teams were waging.

Even as Rockett photographed Arnold's booth, she couldn't help feeling bad for him.

Swinging by, Nicole sneered, "Why are you bothering to shoot him? His campaign is a joke. If he really thinks anyone would vote for him, he's deluded."

Impulsively, Rockett retorted, "Maybe you're deluded. People in this school aren't sheep. It won't automatically be a Ones sweep."

"Oooh, and she rhymes, too!" Nicole snickered, "Try this one: Rockett had to choose? Now Rockett's gonna lose!"

It was Miko who managed to keep everyone focused: "Forget Nicole. Forget Arnold. It's all coming down to the undecideds. We gotta get them."

It was Ruben's music, in the end, that got to Sharla. When Rockett saw her tapping her foot during a lunchtime jam, she seized the moment and approached. Cautiously.

"Ruben's music really kicks, huh?"

Sharla eyed Rockett warily. "And because of that you expect me to vote for you?"

Rockett pursed her lips. "I was hoping so, but not only for that reason. We can change . . ."

Sharla shook her head and started to walk away. "Nothing ever changes. But what the hey, you got my vote. If you care."

111

Rockett was surprised, but pleased. She wasn't sure Sharla even heard her as she called out, "Thanks — you won't regret it!" By that time, Sharla's back was turned, and she was halfway down the corridor.

Feeling confident, Rockett gave Mavis a try during PE. The class did warm-up crunches for the beginning of the period, and Rockett situated herself next to her. Crunches, she noted, were not either of their strong suits.

"Were you, uh, planning to vote?" Rockett asked between grunts.

Mavis responded smoothly, "Why would I? I already know the outcome."

"I'm not saying you can't predict the future . . ." Rockett managed between the fourth and fifth sit-up. "But we should still do what's right, don't you think? And voting is important."

She hadn't realized Darnetta, right behind her, had overheard. "I don't think the founding mothers had junior-high-school elections in mind when they did the whole suffrage thing, you know what I'm sayin'?" Darnetta deadpanned.

Jessie, next to 'Netta, chuckled but sided with Rockett. "Maybe not, but it's the concept — democracy. It's having a voice in your government, even if it's just junior high school."

Mavis exhaled loudly, finished her crunches, and leaned over on her elbow. "Look, Rockett, I'll vote for you, but you know it's a lost cause. Face it, The Ones' 'causes,' whatever you want to call them, are what more people in this school care about. How can you even compare No Homework Fridays to recycling?"

Rockett wished Stephanie had at least wiped the smirk off her face when she happened to pass by just at that moment. She also wished Stephanie hadn't been standing, while they were lying there on the gym floor!

"Hurry up, class, take your seats," Mr. Weaseldorf instructed. "Let's not waste any time. I'm passing out the test papers now — don't forget to write your name at the top of the page, and be sure your numbered answers conform to the questions I've written on the blackboard."

Whitney raised her hand.

"You don't understand something, Ms. Weiss?"

"I can't, uh, see the blackboard too well from where I'm sitting. Can I change my seat?" Whitney pointed to an empty seat — right next to Rockett.

She's gonna look at my paper! I can't believe she'd do it! How obvious can she be, anyway? I should change my seat. No, that's like announcing she's gonna cheat. I can't do that. I should just hunch over so she can't see my paper. But maybe she really can't see the board, and I'm just being ultraparanoid? I should just sit the way I normally do — if she cheats, she cheats. But what if this one test kills her chances at a B average? Should I just let her see my paper on purpose?

CHAPTER TWELVE

Rockett felt nauseous. She'd probably tanked on the test — which meant her first failing grade at Whistling Pines. And not because she was unprepared, or didn't understand the unit. She should have aced it.

But being hyperconscious of Whitney — sitting right next to her the whole time — threw off her concentration. The girl rustled her paper, chewed on her pencil, made loud sighing noises, and, Rockett was pretty sure now, leaned over in her direction several times.

Rockett had not done anything on purpose — neither hunched over to hide her work nor leaned back to allow Whitney a clear view. Either one might have drawn Weaseldorf's attention. So she just did what she normally would — except she totally could not concentrate!

At the bell, she handed in her paper and stalked off in search of Whitney. *That's it — I'm confronting her! How could she put me in this position? I mean, I guess there's a small chance I could be wrong, and if I am, she'll totally hate me. But I can't let this go on, I'm getting too weirded out.*

"Wait up, Whitney! I need to talk to you." Rockett, out of breath, tried to sound nonconfrontational as she caught up to her friend. Who, it seemed, was purposely trying to sprint down the hallway, fast.

"No can do, Rockett."

"Come into the girls' room for one sec, please. I have to ask you something."

"Can't," she explained. "We're doing another round of campaign posters, and I'm already late."

Rockett folded her arms. "You're not leaving me any choice. I'll just come out and say it right here in the hallway: Did you cheat on that test?"

Whitney stopped short. She spun around and frowned. "You're starting to sound like a broken record, Rockett. I know how much you've tried to help me, and I appreciate it, but this is getting psycho. How could you even think I'd do that?"

This time, Rockett wasn't buying Whitney's "best defense is a good offense" strategy. "Well, for starters, you changed your seat to get a better view of my paper!"

"Not even!" Whitney fumed. "I never *wanted* to agree with Nicole, but maybe she's right. You *do* think a lot of yourself! Why would I cheat off you? You said yourself this wasn't your best subject."

"Because," Rockett reminded her, "I know how much getting a good grade means to you. So you might think I'd let you cheat. But you'd be wrong."

Impatiently, Whitney ran her fingers through her frizzy hair. "I think the stress of the whole campaign is getting to both of us. I can see that it's affecting our friendship. I don't want that to happen. So I'll just pretend you don't mean that."

Rockett remained steadfast. "I'm asking you again. Did you cheat?"

"No, Rockett. I did not cheat. But I do declare this conversation *so* over."

Only that wasn't the end of it. As Rockett had feared the two of them were called up to the teacher's desk after social studies the next day.

Mr. Weaseldorf drummed his fingers on the desk and seemed very uncomfortable. He said he was going to get right to the point, only it seemed to take him forever to do so.

"Just so you know, ladies, this is the worst part of my job," he said. "It's so disappointing."

Whitney went into a full fret. "Please don't say I failed! I can't fail!"

The wrinkles on Weaseldorf's forehead deepened. "This is worse. In reviewing your papers, I have reason to believe that there may have been some collusion going on between the two of you."

Whitney blew a fuse. "Collusion? What does that mean? Are you saying we cheated? I mean, how could you say that?"

Weaseldorf hadn't expected Whitney to get defensive. He didn't appreciate it. "A comparison of these test papers is how I could say it. You even crossed out the same answers — right ones, I might add — and wrote in the

116

wrong ones. In all my years of teaching, I've learned to recognize the clues — this is a definite clue."

Whitney maintained her defensive posture. "Did you see us cheating?"

"No, I didn't. If I had, obviously I would have taken steps to stop it right there."

"Well, that proves it!" Whitney was all red. "You didn't see it. And no matter how similar our papers look, you can't mark us down for cheating. That's so unfair!"

Weaseldorf let out a long sigh. "All right, Ms. Weiss. I won't give you a failing grade — this time. But take this as a warning. Somehow, someway, your tests better not ever look this similar again." He turned to Rockett. "You've been awfully quiet, Ms. Movado. Anything to add?"

Rockett felt like she'd split in three. One part of her screamed, "Plenty! She cheated off me and now I'm taking the fall for it!" Another part joined Whitney on the defense. "No way!"

The third part was all Mr. Weaseldorf heard: the sound of silence.

What Whitney heard, the second they were out the door, was Rockett's rage. "How could you do this? You not only cheated, but when I asked you, you lied to me!"

Whitney's anger matched Rockett's. "I didn't! I didn't cheat, and I didn't lie! How could you not believe me?"

"What kind of friend are you, Whitney, to cheat and then lie about it?"

"What kind of friend are you, Rockett — to accuse me and not believe me?"

"Then what was the seat changing thing about?"

"Hello! Like I told you before, I couldn't see the blackboard. Why are you so paranoid? Is it because we're on different teams? I thought this wasn't going to come between us."

"*It* didn't — but I think *you* might have, Whitney."

As if someone had tampered with the thermostat, the temperature in the hallways at Whistling Pines had suddenly plunged. The campaigning kids, at first cool toward one another, were much chillier — and on the way toward frigid.

Rockett knew why Nicole was getting so jumpy. The One saw her landslide victory slipping away. And she didn't like it. When Dana gleefully pointed it out, Nicole snarled, "So you have the random people voting for you — I'm so worried!"

"Yeah," Stephanie parroted, "we have the popular vote."

But it was Max who, on behalf of The Ones, got into trouble. Clearly, the team's campaign manager was concerned enough about the CSG threat to launch a counterattack. He tried to swing votes their way by bribing kids who'd declared for the CSGs. He offered them free tickets to the next college basketball game. He also continued playing poster pranks.

For his efforts, he was given detention.

Mrs. Herrera, her homing device firmly in place, just happened to round the corner, and Max, caught red-handed drawing horns on Ruben's head on a campaign poster, had no excuse.

"Mr. Diamond!" Mrs. Herrera had thundered, so loud that it reverberated off the walls. "To detention. Now!"

When they heard, the CSGs were psyched. Nakili noted. "Good. Shows them they just can't steamroll over us — even if they do have more of a 'war chest.'"

Rockett added, "And even if they are more popular — this should take them down a peg."

Miko ventured, "Now they'll totally be forced to play fair."

Which is why Rockett was completely puzzled when Max, soon after emerging from Mrs. Herrera's office, had a *huge* smile plastered across his face. It was the twinkle in his eye that concerned her even more. She noticed it as he spun around during his "secret huddle" with Nicole. They'd been chatting animatedly, but clammed up the minute Rockett walked by.

Confession Session

I believe that things go my way because, essentially, I'm right. It's not just because I'm popular. It's karma. I never should have doubted our chances of winning. And now, with the note Max "happened to see" on Mrs. H's desk, our winning fate is sealed. The note about a certain someone who's being "investigated" for cheating. A certain someone who had the nerve to pick another team. Did I not, like, warn her that she'd regret it?

CHAPTER THIRTEEN

Because of the debate on Thursday, the last two periods of the day were canceled for the entire eighth grade. Instead, all students filed into the auditorium. Up on the stage, the members of the three parties running for election were seated in folding chairs. A podium was situated in the middle of the stage. Flanking the three teams were Mr. Baldus, who'd "elected" himself moderator, and Principal Herrera.

As soon as everyone was settled, Mr. Baldus walked up to the podium.

"Before we kick off the Great Debate of the Grade of Eight, I want to quote from a great philosopher of our time. Me! 'You can smear your jelly; you can smear your paint, but you can't smear each other in today's great debate!' Now, let's rock 'n' roll — I give you the first principal of Whistling Pines, our very own Mrs. Herrera!"

The principal stood up and explained the procedure. "First we will hear an opening statement from one member of each team. Then each party will address questions submitted by our students. After that, the other teams will get a chance to rebut. So, without further ado, opening statements. A random drawing was held this morning, and the order of speakers will be Nakili Abuto, on behalf of the CSG ticket; Nicole Whittaker, speaking for The Ones; and Arnold Zeitbaum for the Sports."

Arnold's hand shot up.

"Yes, Mr. Zeitbaum? You have a problem?"

Arnold corrected, "It's the Sporks, not the Sports. And I hereby register my objection to going last. I sense a conspiracy."

Mrs. Herrera sighed. "It was a random drawing, Mr. Zeitbaum, I assure you."

Under her breath — but loud enough so everyone on-stage could hear, Nicole muttered, "Last is best, you numbskull. You leave the lasting impression."

Mrs. Herrera shot her a *zip it* look. "I now give you Nakili Abuto."

Nakili, who'd added vintage combs to her hairdo today, confidently approached the podium. With a huge smile, she began, "My fellow students, Mrs. Herrera, Mr. Baldus, and all the teachers of Whistling Pines, the most fly junior high on planet USA! I represent the CSGs, and as you're about to see, we are going to rock this school inside and out! As your elected representatives of our eighth grade, we're going to leave our mark way into the new millennium! Our class will go down in history for making the most improvements in the school, and in our community. We are the right ticket at the right time!"

A wave of applause followed Nakili as she returned to her seat.

"Next," Mr. Baldus announced, "Nicole Whittaker."

Nicole took her time sashaying up to the podium. Rockett was pretty sure she'd never worn heels that high before. Her hair was piled in an updo, giving her a commanding presence. "My friends," she began, "and you *are* my friends — every single one of you! And for that reason alone, The Ones party should be your only choice. But we offer so much more! For we stand for freedom — individual freedom, which, hello, made this country great in the first place. We know what you want — we know what's best for the school. We know what everyone's thinking. We will be your voice. Let us lead."

Then it was Arnold's turn. Head held high, cue cards in his hand, he began, "We all know what's going on here. A mere popularity contest. And I believe, the Sporks believe, you are too smart to fall for that. I urge you to go the less obvious route! Vote Spork!"

"Groovy opening statements," Mr. Baldus complimented the teams. "Now Mrs. Herrera will read the questions submitted by your fellow classmates. And in the interest of fairness, the teachers have not even looked at the questions in advance. They reflect what your classmates are really thinking. Each is directed to one of the parties; then the other two will have the opportunity to rebut."

Armed with a pile of index cards, Mrs. Herrera cleared her throat and began. "Question one, for the CSG team: Your platform includes veggie meals in the cafeteria, but who really cares about rabbit food, aside from one or

125

two . . . zealots?" Frowning, Mrs. Herrera whirled around to speak to the audience. "For whoever wrote this question, rabbit is spelled r-a-b-b-i-t, not r-a-b-i-d. And it's zealots, not z-lots." She turned back to the panels. "Okay, who wants to take that?"

Ruben rose. "I'm the best person to answer that. 'Cause, you know, before I accepted the position on this party, I asked the same thing. But as I delved deeper, I realized, it's not about rabbit food. It's about choice. How would you feel if around noon, you get that grumbling sensation in the stomach that says, 'Feed me, man!' And then you go into the cafeteria, and it's all, like, tongues, intestines, and other weird animal organs that gross you out. And that's all we get, day after day? We gotta feed the world, peeps. Peace out."

Rockett was glowing. Ruben so got it! He got over his own meat-eating thing to see the fairness of everyone getting a choice. Even if he disagreed with it. How cool was that?

Mrs. Herrera had selected The Ones team to go first with their rebuttal. Cleve spoke as if he was bored. "Let's get a *grip*, people. If we had to have stuff every single person likes every single day, you know what the cost would be? We wouldn't have a dime left to throw dances! And what's more important here? Let the one or two devout vegetarians just deal with it. Hey, they made their bed."

Mr. Baldus said, "Rebuttal, Sports . . . I mean, Sporks."

Arnold didn't bother getting up. From his seat, he

said, "It doesn't matter whether they're forcing meat or lettuce at us. It's all a diversionary tactic. Who really knows what's in the food, what's in the water? To be safe, brown-bag it."

Mr. Baldus bounced to his feet. "Okeydokey! Question two, for The Ones party."

Clearly, he really hadn't screened the questions in advance, as he began to scowl halfway through it. "Nicole, where do you . . . buy your ankle-strap platform shoes?" Mr. Baldus turned to Mrs. Herrera, frowning. "We'll eliminate this one."

But Nicole jumped to her feet. "No wait, we *want* to answer — and you'll see how that ties directly in with our campaign pledge. The fact that I can wear what I want brings us to a major issue. For the faculty has banned certain perfectly acceptable clothes groups! Flip-flops, cell phones, these are not just fashion statements, but deeply personal choices. We should be free to make them! Outside these walls, do we not live in a democracy? Should our school not reflect that democracy?" Grinning, she returned to her seat.

"CSG party rebuttal?" Mr. Baldus, scratching his head, invited.

Miko took it. "While The Ones would like to make it seem like a personal choice issue, that clouds the truth. The administration also has a duty to keep us safe. I have statistics here that show how many accidents are caused by kids tripping over their flip-flops as they're running down the hallways or up the stairs. And cell phones dis-

127

tract us from the reason we're in school — to learn. So it's not about choice; it's about education and safety."

When Miko took her seat, Rockett whispered, "You go!"

Mr. Baldus allowed for a Spork rebuttal, but Arnold dismissed it. "I wouldn't even dignify that."

The next question was for the Sporks. Mr. Baldus knew he had to read it — even though he clearly didn't want to. "Which of our teachers is really an alien?"

Arnold let his teammate, Bo, tackle that one. As he mumbled on — stumbling over his words, Rockett couldn't help being distracted by Cleve, who kept nudging Nicole with his knee. If body language could talk, he was all, "I have something to say! Come on, let's get to it." Nicole's return language said, "All in good time. Relax. I know what I'm doing."

Something's up, Rockett fretted. *And I don't like it.*

Mr. Baldus shook his head. "Would either the CSGs or The Ones like to rebut the notion that I am an alien?"

Stephanie rose to speak, but Mrs. Herrera interrupted, "Rhetorical question, Ms. Hollis. You may sit. Now, next question, for The Ones: No Homework Fridays! I'm for that. But does that mean more homework on the other days?"

Whitney answered for her team. "As if! What would be the point, then? We have enough work already. This is the eighth grade, not college. Our education includes going out on Friday night."

Rockett took the CSG rebuttal. "That sounds cool,

but it's an empty promise. It's a popular issue, but just like popular people sometimes, it's shallow. The Ones can't make that happen without the teachers agreeing. So it's an issue that sounds great, but they can't deliver on it."

Arnold's response was, "Diversionary tactic. Who knows what's in the homework?"

"Question for the CSG team," Baldus read. "You say you want to recycle, and who would argue? But you can't force people to do it."

Confidently, Rockett rose. "First we would educate everyone on the importance of recycling. Then it could just be one of our regular school rules. We'd all get used to it in time."

Strangely, Nicole took her sweet time getting to her rebuttal. When she did, she brought the debate to a screeching halt.

"So," she drawled, "Rockett Movado, of all people, wants to talk rules. Well, my friends, this brings us to a very interesting matter. A matter that has only recently come to our attention. Speaking of school rules, there is one major problem the CSG team has — they're breaking them right now!"

The CSGs exchanged confused looks. Nicole attacked. "There's a cheater in their midst! Which automatically cancels them out, if I know the rules for this election." She tossed her hair back. And looked straight at Rockett.

Mr. Baldus and Mrs. Herrera leaped to their feet. "Ms. Whittaker, that's out of line," Mrs. Herrera scolded.

Nicole shrugged. "I don't think so. I have just found out about a person cheating, and since none of the teachers have seen fit to toss her off the team, I see that as my duty. As almost-president-elect of the eighth-grade student body."

In a flash, Nakili was out of her seat. "You better check yourself before you wreck yourself!"

"I suggest you check your own backyard first, Nakili — because Rockett Movado is a cheater!"

Rockett's jaw dropped — so hard she could almost feel it crashing on the floor. "Whaa . . . ?"

"Is it not true, Rockett," Nicole accused, "that you've been called up not once, but twice, on suspicion of cheating! In language arts and in social studies! Once may have been a mistake, but twice? I don't think so!"

Nakili fumed, "She's not on trial, and you're deluded, so stop disrespecting her! And besides, how dare you spring this on us now? When did all this go down?"

Cleve took up the call. "Never mind when it went down, or how we found out. We just did! And now that it's out in the open, we demand that the CSG party concedes defeat, right now, in front of the whole school."

Miko's eyes widened in shock.

Nakili's temper erupted. "As if! Based on your pathetic, desperation-move, whack accusation! I demand YOU concede!"

Whitney seemed to shrink into her chair.

Dana was distressed. And angry. Her expression said it

all: *Rockett has sunk us!* Even Jessie looked upset. Suddenly, the room erupted, and it seemed as if everyone was shouting at the same time.

Only Ruben stayed calm. He got up and squeezed Rockett's shoulder, and whispered in her ear, "Come on, new girl, just tell them it's all bogus!"

Shakily, Rockett stood up. All she heard was thundering. All she saw was a blur. She opened her mouth, but no words came.

She never heard Mrs. Herrera shout, "This debate is officially canceled! Class dismissed! Go to your regular last-period class!"

Although "Class dismissed" really *was* the command given by Mrs. Herrera, apparently what everyone heard was, "What's up with this? Let's go find out!"

A swarm of students rushed the stage. And all at once, Rockett's world was a blur of slo-mo images. For some stupid reason, she felt as if she were swimming through Jell-O and couldn't respond. She heard people shouting, accusing, pointing, saw others with disappointment etched all over their faces. For although no one except the two people involved knew the truth, accusations flew like Frisbees on the front lawn.

The Ones party — with the glaring exception of Whitney — weren't content with their tabloid-esque "exposé" during the debate. In a pack, they circled Rockett, continuing to point the finger of guilt.

"We owe you a huge thanks, Rockett," Nicole

sneered, "for not choosing to go with The Ones party and besmirching *our* reputation!"

Stephanie parroted, "Thanks, Rockett — for handing us the victory, even though we had it all along. This is just icing on the cake."

Cleve, already playing with a yo-yo, added, "I thought I knew you, but you're full of surprises, aren't you?"

Out of the corner of her eye, Rockett saw Arnold. He just kept shaking his head. In spite of the insanity going on around her, Rockett realized there was no joy in the land of the Purple Orchid. On his face, there was just bare-naked concern. And for a split second, deep in her heart, she was touched.

Jessie, trailed by Darnetta, had run up onstage and made her way through the crowd to Rockett's side. But she couldn't get a word in above the yelling. Rockett wasn't sure she wanted to, for Jessie's expression showed extreme upset, not staunch support. She noticed Max, too, hanging by The Ones team, but curiously silent.

The blame-o-rama raged on.

"She stabbed us in the back — we *can't* let it go," Dana pointed out angrily.

But what upset Rockett most was Nakili. Warm, friendly, and above all fair and objective Nakili seemed to turn purple before Rockett's very eyes — Rockett had never seen her this berserk. "What the cheese is going on here, Rockett? A real friend would have told us! You're no friend!"

Rockett felt the chunks coming up in her throat, which rendered her speech-challenged. Two people stood up for her. And *their* declarations were what finally shut down the whole surreal scene.

There was no trace of the soft-spoken, laid-back Ruben when he shouted above the fray, "If jumping to conclusions were an Olympic event, *amigos*, all of you would get the gold! She hasn't even had a chance to defend herself — you could all be wrong!"

That stopped the noise long enough for the second person to be heard. Mavis. "Rockett Movado is innocent. Falsely accused. None of this is true."

Nicole whirled around. Sarcastically, she snapped, "Stop the presses! The psychic Depew has spoken! And just what bogus Ouija board told you this?"

Mavis stood her ground. She didn't even raise her voice. "I didn't need a Ouija board. I know the truth. Rockett Movado is not the problem here. I suggest you look in your own backyard, Nicole."

But if any of The Ones had turned around — which they didn't — they would have found the real culprit was gone. Because Whitney had dashed out the door.

I can't believe this is happening. I have to just scream out that it wasn't me, it was Whitney! I can't let her get away with this! But what if they don't believe me? I knew about it, I should have said something in the first place. That's it, everybody hates me now. Whitney cheated, but I guess I let her.

Confession Session

Why did Rockett let Whitney copy her homework? I warned her against this! Now everyone's screaming — I hate that! Sometimes it's so hard to be Rockett's friend.

CHAPTER FOURTEEN

Though the fight the next morning was coming from behind the door of the girls' room, the volume was turned up to ear-shattering, making it impossible for any-one in the school hallway not to hear. Including Rock-ett, who'd been standing kind of nervously just outside the door.

Nicole was pitching a championship hissy fit. That you couldn't see the victim was a moot point: for the gossip-spreading grapevine had, again, done an A-plus job.

Whitney Weiss was in deep trouble with her best friend, and everyone knew it.

"How could you do this to me? Behind my back — you betrayed me! You're lower than a slug — and just as spineless!" The high and mighty One screeched, way out of control.

Practically anyone else in the entire school would have flown out of the girls' room. That, or broken down in sobs.

But Whitney held her ground. She growled, "Tough concept, but try wrapping it around your brain, Ni-cole: It's not *about* you! It's about me — and . . ." Whit-ney faltered only slightly. "It was time I did the right thing."

"Right thing for who? For my ticket? For my candidacy? You are beyond selfish!"

Angry now, Whitney shot back, "If you'd told me that Max saw a note in Mrs. Herrera's office, this wouldn't have happened! I would have told you that Rockett wasn't cheating — I was! So the whole thing is *your* fault! You and your stupid secrets!"

"Oh, right! Turn the tables on me. I don't think so. With stab-in-the-back friends like you, who needs mortal enemies?"

"If anyone's not a friend, it's you! You are so self-centered! You have no clue! I just wanted to see my mother . . ." *Whomp* — that was it. The floodgates had opened and Whitney broke down in tears.

And this time, Rockett had no choice: She burst into the girls' room.

She didn't even have to say anything: Supportively, she sided with Whitney, and handed her a tissue.

Whitney blew her nose. "I was just coming to tell you, Rockett. I wanted to do it in person. After the debate, I went to Mrs. Herrera. And I told her the whole story. All of it. How I copied your homework, and then pretended I didn't. How I cheated off you in social studies, and then . . . denied it. I know this doesn't make it right, but I was desperate — and . . . you were . . . trying to be a friend. But, anyway, now Mrs. Herrera knows that you had nothing to do with it. I'm sorry."

Rockett put her arm around Whitney. "I know. I heard."

In fact, the whole school had. Overnight — via phone and E-mail — word had spread faster than the Ebola virus. The first call Rockett got was from Nakili, who apologized big-time for "ever doubting you, girl. I should've believed you when you said you had nothing to do with it. I should've listened to my heart."

Gladly, Rockett had forgiven her. "I should have told you about being called up by Mrs. Tinydahl and Mr. Weaseldorf. I wasn't cheating, but I knew that they were reporting their suspicions to Mrs. Herrera. It's just that I felt bad for Whitney — and I didn't want to rat her out."

"Nuff said, Rockett," Nakili replied. "Standing by a friend: We've all been there."

After that, Rockett heard from Jessie, who'd heard from Darnetta, who'd heard from Chaz, who apparently had gotten the word from Max: He's the one Whitney called.

Only two people, it seemed, hadn't heard: Nicole, who'd spent the evening at her grandmother's. And Stephanie, who'd gone with her.

Nicole's finding out just now, on Friday morning, was a major event — it had everyone enthralled. And if nothing else, Nicole had made *that* spectator-worthy.

She was spitting bullets. "Look at this sweet little scene, would you? The two of you, such good friends! I'm so over both of you!"

With that, she flew out the door in a rage. Stephanie, who'd been there, too, but was stunned into silence, paused. She looked at Whitney and Rockett, and then at

Nicole's quickly retreating form. Torn for only a split second, Steph sped out the door after Nicole.

Later, Rockett would think, *And the award for Best Performance by a Schemer goes to . . . Nicole Whittaker.* For somewhere between her girls' room temper tantrum and her tardy arrival to homeroom, Nicole had managed to formulate a plan.

It took Mr. Baldus only slightly longer than usual to get the class to quiet down. At the front of the room, he bellowed for everyone to "cease and desist the chattering! I hear ya! I know everyone's buzzing about the wild 'n' woolly events of yesterday's great debate. And it *was* a great debate — you know why? I'll tell you why! Because it took us to the truth!"

Rockett and Ruben next to her groaned in tandem — they instinctively knew that Baldus, now launched, was about to crash-land on planet Cliché. They were right.

"The truth, my friends, is stranger than fiction! Truth is always served by great minds, even if they fight it! The truth shall set us free!" Grinning wildly, he continued, "It *has* set us free, free to rock 'n' roll! 'Cause it's gonna take more than one little speed bump to stop the flow of democracy here in this great junior high school of ours!"

It was Max who called out, "Your *point*? Yo, Mr. B, let's get to it."

Baldus obliged. "An emergency meeting of the administration was called, and here, my friends, is how it's gonna play out. In light of the situation, Ms. Whitney

Weiss has done the honorable thing and stepped down from the ticket."

At that, all heads swirled around to Whitney, who was sitting in the back of the room. A pained yet slightly proud look was on her face. Her eyes were still a little puffy from crying.

"The Ones ticket," Mr. Baldus described, "will have two days to fill the vacated slot of vice president. Then, on Wednesday a brief debate will be held — to remind everyone of those super-duper issues. After which, we vote! Our class election will only be a trifle tardy."

As if on cue, Nicole slipped into the room. She raised her hand while walking to her seat. And before being recognized, she announced, "We won't need two days. It will be handled by the end of the day."

"It will?" Even Stephanie looked stunned.

"Leave it to me. I promise," Nicole assured Mr. Baldus and the class — who, clearly, she thought of as her constituents. "The Ones will be back, stronger than ever!"

Nicole was good as her word. Better even.

For, given her popularity, it wasn't too surprising that by the end of the day, she'd snagged a volunteer to fill Whitney's spot on The Ones ticket. It was *who* she got that rattled the competition: Wolf DuBois. The independent, lone Wolf had never before been known to care much about class elections. And now, just because Nicole asked him, he agreed to be in the middle of one?

140

"What's *that* about?" Rockett had voiced the major concern on everyone's mind during an emergency meeting of the CSG party.

"Wish I knew." Ruben sighed and scratched his head.

"Well, I do," Dana grumbled, crossing her arms over her chest. "Nicole just batted her eyelashes. She always gets what she wants."

Gravely, Nakili noted, "This development could bring new voters The Ones' way. Kids who like Wolf — and that's a lot."

"And doesn't Nicole know it," Miko said, not in the form of a question.

"What should we do?" Rockett asked.

Decisively, Nakili said, "As team leader, I say we stick to our platform. We change nothing, just remind people who we are and what we stand for. We're solid."

Because The Ones had not needed the allotted two days to fill Whitney's spot, Mrs. Herrera decided that the follow-up mini-debate could be moved up. She scheduled it for the next day at two P.M., after which the votes would be cast. The principal explained, "Each party will once again remind the class of your issues. You will each address one question submitted by students, with rebuttals to follow. And I warn everyone this time — no surprises!"

The CSGs were ready. Their question — "Will there be a CD of the songs Ruben played during the campaign?" — was answered by a totally thrilled Ruben.

The Spork party was ready. Their question — "Will there be a class — that is, cup/glass — to go along with the Spork? Or blate — a bowl/plate?" — was answered by an impressed Arnold.

The Ones were beyond ready. Which made Rockett suspect they'd somehow planted their question; that's how ready they were to make their point.

Mr. Baldus read, "'If you didn't even know someone on your team was cheating, what makes you qualified to lead us?'"

Nicole smoothed her skirt carefully and took her sweet time approaching the podium. In a tone of voice that, for her anyway, approached humble — *What an actress!* Rockett thought — she said, "We so deeply regret the events of the past few days. It is true that someone on our team, under unbearable stress, was making the wrong choices. Yet we don't assign blame. Instead we accept responsibility."

Arnold seemed to snort his rebuttal. "Am I the only one who sees it? The lady doth protest too much! She may be fair of face, and clever of prose, but do not let her blind you to the truth, I implore you. Focus on the mighty Spork, for it represents simplicity, economy, the one simple truth: You need me to lead you into the future. I am the only qualified one!"

Nakili took the high road. "Let's give Nicole a thumbs-up, 'cause the girl's got skills. Acting skills. And oratory skills: Sounds like she's sayin' somethin', when the real is, she's got nothing on her brain but herself.

Let's give her a thumbs-down! And while your thumbs are down, hit the button that says CSG on the voting computer. 'Cause we're in it for the long haul, and Whistling Pines is gonna be better for it. You know it: Vote your hearts!"

The actual voting was held in the computer lab, where special software had been installed on the school's PCs and Macs. All during seventh and eighth periods, students filed in to cast their E-ballots. Mrs. Herrera, Mr. Baldus, Mrs. Tinydahl, and Mr. Weaseldorf took turns monitoring, making sure that each eighth grader got to vote in private — and didn't go back in line to another computer to vote again.

"I wonder if that had something to do with Max," Rockett remarked to Jessie. The girls had decided to go into computer lab together. "I thought I heard him 'suggesting' that maybe The Ones' supporters could find a way to, you know, vote more than once."

Jessie tensed. Sternly, she said, "Max would never do that."

Rockett frowned. *She can't really be defending Max, right? Why would she? This is about me. What Jessie means is that I wouldn't know a cheater if I tripped over one. I bet she's saying why didn't I listen to her and Darnetta. I should just tell her to come out and say it — 'cause sometimes Jessie can seem so sweet even when she's really not. But that might make her mad. And I don't know if I want to risk that.*

* * *

143

At the end of the official school day, Mrs. Herrera and the teachers would compile the computer printouts of the votes. Winners were set to be announced by seven P.M. that night. Anyone interested enough to hear the results right away could come to the school, which would remain open until eight P.M.

As a team, the CSGs decided to wait out the election results in the art classroom. Their supporters were invited to hang with them. Ruben's band mates, Olivia, Lar-Dog, and Ian, showed up, as did Arrow, Ginger, and Viva. Unbeknownst to Rockett until that day, they'd decided to form a superjam and play together if — that is, when — the CSGs won.

"That is so cool!" Rockett exclaimed when Arrow told her. It was beyond cool, when she realized she could count her own friends in the room. Jessie and Darnetta were there, Mavis made an appearance, even Sharla, although she pretty much spent the time with her back pressed against the wall.

Thanks to Nakili, a total party atmosphere prevailed. She'd arranged for a victory celebration. Aside from the music, there was food, balloons, confetti, even noisemakers.

And attitude. "It's in the bag," Nakili would respond every time someone wished her team good luck.

As she moved easily among the different conversations, Rockett was totally glowing. *This is the best time I've had at Whistling Pines since the day I got here. I'm so all about being part of a team! And the coolest part? If we*

144

win — *that is, when we win* — *I get to stay on the team with my friends. We'll spend the whole rest of the year totally hanging together, representing the eighth grade. But if we . . . uh, don't win, I guess things will go back to the way they were before. Which isn't bad . . . just not as good.*

"So, Rockett." Miko tapped her on the arm, interrupting her train of thought. "Are you as nervous as I am? I'm totally eating everything in sight! That's how goosey-crazy I am. I wish we had the results now."

Rockett grinned. "Chill, Miko. Like Nakili says, 'It's in the bag.'"

Miko bit her lip. "But don't you think The Ones are saying the same exact thing?"

Rockett nodded. She knew that The Ones felt just as upbeat, assured of success. They, too, were holding a "previctory" celebration. Only not at the school. Though they planned to return in time for the big announcement, they were congregating at their hangout, Let's Get Some 'Za.

She could just picture Nicole terrorizing the wait-staff; Cleve flirting with every girl in the place; Max boasting about their definite win. What she couldn't picture was if Whitney was with them. Or if Whitney ended up banned from The Ones — home alone.

Maybe I should call her? What would I say, exactly? If I invited her to hang with us, would she? But what if she says no — she's still a One. Wouldn't I feel lame? But then again, wouldn't a true friend just pick up the phone?

Suddenly, Mavis ambled over, joining Rockett and

Miko. "Nice-size crowd you got here supporting you, Rockett," Mavis noted.

Miko eyed Mavis mischievously. "Should we even ask you for a prediction?"

Mavis rolled her eyes. "No, you shouldn't. But I'll say this much. You can eliminate the Sporks. They're no competition to anyone. For anything."

Arnold and his Sporks. Rockett sighed, unsure where he was. Or if he even had people to be with. Bo Pezanski, in the end, had pretty much deserted Arnold. He'd been at the second debate but hadn't said a word, just sat there with a bored expression. Rockett guessed he wasn't even around tonight.

When, at precisely seven P.M., Rockett heard the static rustle of the PA system, she wasn't ready for it. "Wow! They're really on time here," she exclaimed, her stomach starting to churn.

"Good evening, students!" Mrs. Herrera's voice came over loud and clear. "I am proud and happy to say that, in spite of recent turmoil here at Whistling Pines, the election process has come through unsullied!"

"This is it!" Nakili yelled, excited. "The moment we've all been waiting for! Get ready to raise the roof!"

"Oh! No!" Miko nearly shook. "Let's hold hands!"

"No way, *chica*," Ruben shouted. "Let's make some noise!" With that, he started to blow hard on a noise-maker.

Over the PA system, Mrs. Herrera was saying, "All the

146

votes have been counted, and the new officers of the student government of Whistling Pines are . . . drumroll please!"

It's us! I know it's us! I'm going to run up and hug Ruben! No, I better not. I mean, how would I feel if he didn't hug me back? Or worse, turned around and hugged Arrow or someone? I'd just be standing there, with my arms out, looking lame. No, when they announce our name, I'm going to hug Nakili! Or . . . wait. I have a better idea. The minute she says, "The CSG party," I'm going to bury the hatchet for good and hug Dana! Of course, that could be another huge mistake: What if Dana disses me? That would spoil everything.

CHAPTER FIFTEEN

"The Ones party!"

Because Ruben was blowing so hard on his noise-maker, and because Rockett was so sure Mrs. Herrera had said "The CSG Party!" she'd actually thrown her arms open and run up to . . . Dana. Which is why she felt lame-squared when it hit her, like a ton of bricks: That's not what Mrs. H had said at all.

Had the art room gone all surrealistic, or were those student paintings on the walls, imitating Chagall, Dalí, or Picasso in his blue period, a sign they all missed? For the weirdest thing happened. Dana, seeing Rockett's ready embrace, rushed over and hugged *her*. Not in joy-ous victory — but in total devastation. Her voice choked, "I can't believe this, Rockett. How could we lose?"

Rockett wanted more than anything to say the right thing. The thing that would make Dana accept her as Nakili and Miko had. But she was too bummed to think straight. So all that came out was, "I don't know, Dana, I . . ."

And snap, Dana was back to herself, raging, "This stinks! I bet it was rigged! I demand . . ."

"A recount!" The voice that ended Dana's sentence

belonged to someone who wasn't even on their team. Arnold Zeitbaum had just blasted into the art room, arms waving, hat-hair spiked, fully wigging out.

And like a bucket of ice water splashed on a beautiful dream, the mood in the art classroom crashed from sky-high to the ocean bottom. Dana, eyes flashing, stomped over to Arnold. In their fury, the two actually bonded. The whole room heard them prattling about a wide-ranging "conspiracy."

Where there should have been music, this amazing jam session, there stood six mannequins: Ruben and his Rebel Angels, plus Arrow, Viva, and Ginger, all with noisemakers, their instruments unplugged. There was no victory for their victory jam.

When Jessie darted up to Rockett, oozing with real sympathy, Rockett was glad she'd decided not to confront her about the Whitney remark. Jessie really was a good person. A good friend.

Rockett saw that depression threatened to overtake Miko, whose shoulders seemed to cave inward. Mavis stood next to her, with what Rockett knew to be words of comfort.

Nakili broke the bummer-spell. Like a born leader, their shoulda-been president marched up to the front of the classroom and rapped loudly on the blackboard with Mr. Rarebit's pointer. When that failed to get everyone's attention, she grabbed a noisemaker and blew hard.

That did it.

"I want to thank each and every one of you for your

support," Nakili, head high, announced. "Maybe we didn't get enough votes, maybe the whole thing was rigged, I don't know. But I do know this. We did the right thing. We have the best people here in this room. And we're gonna continue to fight for the things we want. That's how it works. We're never gonna give up. So stop acting like this is some kind of memorial service — let's crank it up and par-tay!"

Because people had started to cheer Nakili, no one saw Nicole until she'd opened the classroom door all the way and stood there, framed in the doorway, gloating big-time. Just as Ruben and Arrow were about to start playing, she shouted, "What's this? A loser party! Kudos on the novel concept — of course, those are the only kudos you get tonight!"

It was Max, of all people, who grabbed her elbow and pulled her away. "Give it a rest, Nicole."

Rockett didn't see the glance exchanged between him and someone else in the room. If she had, a lot would have been made clear.

Nicole and her team must have worked all night, Rockett thought when she got to school the next morning. For The Ones and their supporters were stationed in all the corridors, passing out invitations. New posters adorned the walls. All advertised the same thing: CELEBRATE! THE ONES PARTY INVITES ONE AND ALL TO A VICTORY PARTY! FUN, GAMES, SNACKS, AND MUSIC — BE ON THE SOCCER FIELD AFTER SCHOOL TODAY!

* * *

And at the appointed hour, the whole school, it seemed to Rockett, showed up. Hundreds of kids, from grades six, seven, and eight, plus all the teachers, poured outside onto the soccer field. Not a one was disappointed.

Long tables had been set up smorgasbord-style, piled with food. When Rockett saw the banners hanging from them, she was surprised. They read, CATERING BY DUBOIS. Wolf's parents, who owned a restaurant, and some of their wait-staff were behind the tables, cheerfully ladling out the food. They'd even supplied coolers filled with drinks.

A makeshift stage had been erected where one of the goalposts usually stood. On it, a deejay station had been set up, along with a microphone. Joining Nicole, Cleve, Stephanie, and Max onstage, but looking majorly uncomfortable, was Wolf, who hung back just a bit. And one other person: Whitney Weiss. Looking every bit a One — every bit as if she belonged.

Nicole made the most of her moment in the sun. Even Rockett had to admit that Nicole looked really good, regal even. She grabbed the mike, and the spotlight, and launched into her victory speech.

Ringing the stage were The Ones' supporters, and many of the teachers, including Mr. Baldus, Mr Barebit, and Mrs. Herrera.

Rockett stood nearby, next to Nakili, Miko, and Dana. The latter had gotten over her bonding-with-

Arnold moment. And Miko had recovered from her brief bout with the blues. The CSGs were resigned, but resolved, as Nakili had urged, to continue to fight for what they wanted.

Nicole's victory speech was entirely predictable. "Just like her," Rockett remarked to Miko, who agreed vigorously. "Full of empty promises and hooray-for-us hype."

"We look forward to doing so much for the school! We're going to fight for flip-flops! And cell phones! And while we're waging the war for freedom of clothes-choice I have a major announcement. I'm thrilled to announce that the date for the eighth-grade trip has been selected."

There seemed to be some unspoken signal among the CSGs to leave. Nakili, Miko, and Dana walked away. Rockett could have said, "Wait up, guys." They hadn't really meant to leave her out, had they? But Rockett did want to hear this part: The class trip had been the only Ones issue she was psyched about.

Nicole was describing, "Next month, as promised, we will board charter buses and head off to the best city with the best shopping in the world, Chicago, USA!"

Mrs. Herrera's voice suddenly boomed above Nicole's. "I don't want to interrupt, President Whittaker, but may I remind you, this will be an educational trip, not a shopping spree. Now, please continue your speech."

Someone tapped Rockett on the arm. "Don't know about you, new girl, but I've heard enough. That Nicole is in a class by herself." Ruben had sidled up to her. Rock-

152

ett couldn't hide a huge grin, or the beginnings of a blush.

"You got that right," Rockett agreed.

"Wanna hit the smorgasbord? You up for a hot dog?"

Rockett knew Ruben was purposely teasing her. About the hot dog, that is. "I could definitely go for a snack, pasta salad or something."

Ruben laughed as they turned away from the stage and started toward the food line. "Forgot who I was talking to, veggie-girl."

"No, you didn't, you just like to tease me."

Ruben's eyes twinkled. "Me, tease? Nah, never happen." They reached the food, and Ruben loudly joked, "I'll have one *meaty* hot dog!"

Rockett giggled while filling a small paper bowl with a scoop of pasta salad.

All at once, Rockett needed to get serious. "I never got to thank you for standing up for me at that first debate, when Nicole accused me of cheating."

Ruben's tone matched her somber one. "I know what it's like to be bruised for no reason, Rockett."

"What . . . do you mean?"

But if Ruben was about to open up, he must have changed his mind, just like that, because he said, "Look, new girl, it wasn't right for all of them to accuse you. You're not like that."

Rockett hoped he'd say more — about her — but Ruben's mind had jumped to someone else. He spun around toward the stage and pointed at Wolf. "My man looks *muy* uncomfortable up there."

"Did you ever find out why he agreed to join Nicole?"

"I did. And I kinda get it, too."

"Is it because he has a crush on her, too?"

If Ruben got the implications of "too" he didn't let on. "Can't comment on that, except you gotta admit, sometimes Nicole really has got it goin' on. If she could just check her personality at the door!"

Ping! Rockett's heart didn't exactly break, but she felt the pinch. Then Ruben added, "Anyway, Wolf did have at least one practical reason. He's big-time into his folks' restaurant. And Nicole promised that she'd steer more kids toward the place. That's why they're here, catering this whole shebang."

"I get it."

Suddenly, without warning, Ruben casually slipped his arm around Rockett's waist and whispered, "Anyway, it's all *muy* complicated. I'm gonna get over to the stage and make sure Mr. Deejay person plays something real."

As Rockett watched him leap onto the stage, she regarded Whitney, her arm casually tossed around Cleve's shoulder, laughing joyously. Back in the land of the superficial. After all that. As if nothing had happened.

I should just follow Ruben, leap up there, and talk to her. I mean, in the end, Whitney did the right thing. She proved we're friends. It wouldn't seem weird for me to go up. But . . . me? In a sea of Ones? I don't know if I could do

154

that. What if she turns into the old Whitney and ignores me? How pathetic will I feel then? And everybody in the crowd below would see me standing there.

For a split second, Rockett stood paralyzed. It was Ruben's glance, and his wave from up on the stage where he was huddling with the deejay, that gave Rockett the courage to approach Whitney.

She had to admit, though, to being completely relieved when Whitney turned away from Cleve and greeted her warmly. "Hey, Rockett! I'm soooo psyched that you're here — no hard feelings."

Rockett smiled, but crossed her arms and whispered, "Riddle me this, Whitney, how could you get back with them so quickly, I mean, after everything that happened?"

Whitney motioned for Rockett to step away from the clutch of Ones. Then she shrugged. "I know it must seem weird to you, but it's like, Nicole and I have a zillion fights. We always make up — that's what friends do."

Rockett frowned, unconvinced. "But they used you, Whitney. You don't mind?"

Clearly, she didn't. "We all use each other sometimes, don't you think?"

Whitney rushed on. "And anyway, there's more. Nicole told me this in confidence, so don't spread it around. Wolf agreed to take my place temporarily. Just to get elected. Then, he might step down! By that time, I will have taken all the makeup tests, and I can be eligible to get back on the ticket."

"That's so manipulative!" Rockett blurted without thinking.

"Whatever. But here's the best part, Rockett. I've been meaning to tell you. I followed the advice you gave me."

"Advice? About what?"

"About talking to my dad — don't you remember? I just told him how stressed this whole thing about the trip had made me, and how it even made me resort to cheating. And how ashamed I was, especially the way things ended up."

"What'd he say?"

"Well, he was so proud of me for coming clean that I'm getting to go on the trip after all!"

And in spite of everything that had happened, Rockett was majorly psyched for Whitney. Her jaw dropped and she hugged her friend. "That's great! Whitney, I'm so happy for you."

"Yeah, it feels like I went through this major black tunnel, but now I'm out and everything's sunny again. I'm back with them, and in spite of everything? I like being popular. And for a while there, Rockett, when you were in the middle of things, you did, too."

Rockett paused. "Well, okay, but I wouldn't want to be popular for the wrong reasons, like because of who I'm friends with."

"I know."

Rockett was startled. "You do?"

"Uh-huh. That's why people *like* you, Rockett, 'cause you do your own thing. In this school, that's pretty brave."

"Well, you were pretty brave, too, Whitney. To tell the truth after all that."

Whitney grinned and slipped her arm through Rockett's. "Okay, so let's make a pact. Regardless of who our friends are, we can still be friends, right?"

At that second, out of the corner of her eye, Rockett spied someone else. Someone who wasn't on the stage with them, but pretty far back in the crowd. "Right, Whitney. I gotta go, see you later."

Rockett jumped off the stage and made her way through the crowd until she reached Jessie.

"Hey, you!" Rockett greeted her.

"Right back atcha," Jessie said. "I was watching you up there. Wish you'd made the choice to go with them?"

"Not for a second, Jess."

Jessie didn't say a word; her look said it all. Suddenly Rockett remembered something. She tilted her head. "In all the craziness, I forgot to ask you. Did you ever find out who your secret admirer was?"

Jessie blushed; her eyes darted to the ground for a second. "I did."

"Jessie! Give it up!" Rockett commanded.

Biting her lip, Jessie looked up slowly. And pointed to the stage — but Rockett didn't get it. Until slowly it all dawned on her. There had been lots of clues, especially

Jessie's staunch defense of Max when Rockett accused him of "suggesting" The Ones' supporters vote more than once.

Her hand flew to her mouth. "Max? Max Diamond, The One?"

"You think you're the only person not in their clique who can have . . . let's say . . . a *friend* who is?"

Ouch. Guilty as charged. But determined to fess up and deal honestly, Rockett apologized and gushed, "Jessie, that's so . . . cool. Tell me all about it. Every detail."

So, as Nicole and The Ones continued to commandeer the stage and gloat about their win, the music played on — and Rockett listened completely as her friend Jessie dished.

And best of all — Rockett's spirits soared. For her friend and for herself.

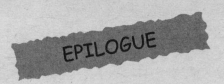

EPILOGUE

Wow! That was totally my most amazing time at Whistling Pines. Not everything turned out the way I wanted. And maybe I made some off-the-hook decisions. But I've got tons to look forward to.

Especially the school trip. Not only are we going to Chicago, but I found out that it's an overnight! What could be more fun than that?

CONFESSION SESSION

ABOUT THE AUTHOR

Lauren Day: Pseudonym-alert! My real name is Randi Reisfeld and I've written lots of books for teens and 'tweens. Maybe you've read some. I've done a bunch in the *Clueless* series (based on the classic movie and TV show); the *Moesha* series; *Meet the Stars of Animorphs*; and *Prince William: The Boy Who Will Be King*, to cite a few that are circa now. Then there's *Got Issues Much? Celebrities Share Their Traumas and Triumphs*, where today's top young stars tell how they got through the tough times. Landing in *Rockett's World* is my coolest writing gig so far — I hope you come along for all the journeys.

You've read all about Rockett and the Whistling Pines kids,

now really hang out with them.

What's so cool is that every Purple Moon CD-ROM friendship adventure in the Rockett series has all the same smart, funny, and sometimes outrageous (uh . . . Nicole) characters as this book. Plus, all the action in the CD-ROM adventures takes place in the same Whistling Pines world, too. Talk about the ultimate way to become even better friends with Rockett and her crowd.

Meet me at

Purple Moon

www.purple-moon.com

For more information on Purple Moon products, visit your favorite software retailer.

HADRIAN
THE SEVENTH

A Play

by

PETER LUKE

SAMUEL FRENCH

LONDON

NEW YORK   SYDNEY   TORONTO   HOLLYWOOD

HADRIAN THE SEVENTH

First produced by the Birmingham Repertory Theatre on 9th May 1967 and subsequently at the Mermaid Theatre, London E.C.4, on the 18th April 1968, with the following cast of characters:

(in order of their appearance)

FR. WILLIAM ROLFE	Alec McCowen
MRS CROWE	Margaret Courtenay
FIRST BAILIFF	Alan MacNaughtan
SECOND BAILIFF	Donald Eccles
AGNES	Peggy Aitchison
DR TALACRYN, BISHOP OF CAERLEON	Alan MacNaughtan
DR COURTLEIGH, CARDINAL-ARCHBISHOP OF PIMLICO	Donald Eccles
JEREMIAH SANT	Patrick McAlinney
THE CARDINAL-ARCHDEACON	William Bond
FATHER ST ALBANS, PREPOSITOR-GENERAL OF THE JESUITS	Brian Tully
CARDINAL BERSTEIN	Otto Diamant
CARDINAL RAGNA	Brian Coburn
RECTOR OF ST ANDREW'S COLLEGE	Aidan Turner
GEORGE ARTHUR ROSE	Vivian Mackerrell
PAPAL CHAMBERLAIN	Patrick Marley
CARDINALS	Anthony King, Graham Leaman, Clifford Norgate, Jeffrey Sacks, John C. Wright
SEMINARISTS	Roger Clayton, Alan Helm, Laurence Terry
PAPAL GUARDS	David Ralph, Edmund Thomas
SWISS GUARDS	Roger Clayton, Alan Helm, Anthony King, Christopher Masters, Jeffrey Sacks, Laurence Terry
ACOLYTES	Roger Clayton, Alan Helm, Christopher Masters, David Ralph, Laurence Terry, Edmund Thomas

The Play directed by PETER DEWS

Settings by Tim Goodchild

ACT ONE

ACT TWO

Time—around 1903

A NOTE ON THE APPEARANCE AND BEHAVIOURISMS OF ROLFE/HADRIAN

Frederick William Rolfe, when the play opens, is a smallish, spare man, of about forty. He wears his greying hair very short, is myopic and can hardly see without his plain, steel-rimmed spectacles, but he is slim, agile and erect.

His tastes are austere but he is fond of such things as goat's milk, apples, raw carrots, fresh linen and particularly water, both to drink and to wash in. He is a practical man and carries a penknife with which he prepares his apples, sharpens pencils, etc.

He smokes a lot, always rolling his own and tucking the ends in with a pencil. Cat-like, his movements are swift, lithe and silent. Likewise, there are moments when he remains utterly still. As Pope, he comports himself with extraordinary dignity when the occasion demands, though 'off-duty' he reverts to his more abnormal self. In the early part of Act I and at the end of the play, Rolfe wears a threadbare clerical grey suit. During the rest of the play, Rolfe/Hadrian wears such Canonical dress as may be appropriate.

ACT I

SCENE 1

SCENE—*A corner of Frederick Rolfe's bed-sitting room in London.*
The room is the abode of a poor scholar of fastidious habits and austere tastes. There is a small gas-fire R, the meter for which is on the wall down R. Up L is the door leading to the rest of the house. A small chest-of-drawers is up C, and below it a wooden armchair. Religious painting covers the walls, and there is a small crucifix on the wall below the fire. Next to the gas meter is a mirror. A wooden chair is wedged beneath the door-handle. Books lie around, and there is a bottle of ink on the floor below the armchair.

When the CURTAIN *rises,* ROLFE *is seated in the armchair writing a manuscript on his knees, and smoking a fat, untidy rolled cigarette which he seldom takes out of his mouth. He is shivering with cold, and has a blanket wrapped around him. After a moment there is a knock on the door.* ROLFE *looks round to make sure the chair is firmly wedged in place and smirks with satisfaction. The knocking is repeated more peremptorily, accompanied by rattlings of the door-handle.*

MRS CROWE (*off*) Mr Rolfe. (*She tries the handle, which does not give*) Mr Rolfe! (*She rattles the handle*) What's the matter with this door? Mr Rolfe, I know you're there.

ROLFE. Tickle your ass with a feather, Mrs Crowe.

MRS CROWE (*off*) What did you say?

ROLFE. Particularly nasty weather, Mrs Crowe.

MRS CROWE (*off*) Mr Rolfe, I haven't climbed all these stairs just to be insulted. There are two gentlemen below who wish to see you.

ROLFE (*starting up; noticeably startled*) To see *me*?

MRS CROWE (*off*) Yes, to see you.

(ROLFE *quickly takes the fag-end out of his mouth and moves to the door to remove the barricade.* MRS CROWE *enters furiously. She is a widow of about forty with pretentions to good looks and gentility. She succeeds only in being "genteel".* ROLFE *looks nervously past her down the staircase*)

Ah, I thought you'd come off your high horse when you heard that

ROLFE (*recovering slightly*) Oh—well, I'm very busy. (*He puts the chair* L *of the door*)

MRS CROWE. They said it was a private matter which couldn't wait.

ROLFE (*attempting to bluster*) I'm not prepared to see them unless they state the precise nature of their business, Mrs Crowe.

Mrs Crowe. If you think I'm going to run all the way up and down these stairs like a skivvy to carry your messages . . . (*Significantly*) I think you'd better see them, Mr Rolfe.

Rolfe. Oh? Hmmm! Very well. Please show them up, Mrs Crowe, but let it be understood—

(Mrs Crowe *exits, shutting the door*)

—that I haven't got all day. (*Crossing to the mirror*) Lascivious bitch! (*He quickly takes a stiff white collar and a plain black tie from the chest-of-drawers and puts them on. He hastily puts a packet of oatmeal out of sight in a drawer, then sits and makes notes on his manuscript*) I'm in an awful state. Come on, come on, buck up. (*Hearing footsteps*) Oh, my God . . .

(*There is the sound of footsteps mounting the stairs, and with a peremptory knock* Mrs Crowe *ushers in the two Bailiffs. The* Second Bailiff *is a venerable-looking old man with white hair. His colleague, the* First Bailiff, *is a tall, amiable, healthy-looking fellow in his early forties. It is suggested that they should bear a resemblance to Dr Courtleigh, Cardinal-Archbishop of Pimlico, and Dr Talacryn, Bishop of Caerleon respectively. Alternatively, the parts can be doubled to emphasise the likeness.* Rolfe *goes on making notes. After a moment he looks up*)

(*Turning on the charm*) Ah, good-day, gentlemen. (*With a gracious nod to Mrs Crowe*) Thank you so much, Mrs Crowe. (*He rises and moves* R)

(Mrs Crowe *hovers in the hope of hearing something*)

Please don't bother to wait. I shall see my visitors out myself.

(Mrs Crowe *exits reluctantly.* Rolfe *draws himself up to the full extent of his inconsiderable height to receive his guests. A trembling knee alone gives away his nervousness*)

And now, gentlemen, please tell me how I can be of service to you.

First Bailiff (*looking at a document in his hand*) Are you Mr Corvo?

Rolfe (*suspiciously*) No.

First Bailiff (*looking at his papers*) Sorry, sir. I mean *Baron* Corvo?

Rolfe. That is not my name.

First Bailiff (*consulting his papers*) Oh. Then are you Frank W. Hochheimer?

(*The* Second Bailiff *sits in the chair* L)

Rolfe (*stiffly*) No.

First Bailiff. Or Mr F. Austin?

Rolfe (*icily*) I am not.

Second Bailiff. But you *are* Mr Frederick William Rolfe (*he pronounces it as in "golf"*) are you not, sir?

ROLFE. That is almost correct. My name is Frederick William *Rolfe.* (*He pronounces it as in* "oaf") And who, may I ask, are you?

FIRST BAILIFF. My colleague and I are Officers of the Court— Bailiffs, you understand—and we hold a writ against you, Mr Rolfe (*handing the writ to Rolfe*) on behalf of certain parties—

(ROLFE *takes the writ and reads it*)

—claiming certain debts. Do you follow me so far, Mr Rolfe?

ROLFE. Your brevity will assist my comprehension.

FIRST BAILIFF. Quite so, sir. And I'm sure my colleague and I have no wish to remain here longer than necessary, so I will endeavour to constrict myself to the essential details, sir. The position is that, in brief, the Court has seen fit to award against you the initial sum of the debt plus the costs of the several plaintiffs versus Yourself for which a remittance must be made into Court forthwith in default of which and in consideration of a Warrant of Execution there will be no alternative but to attend at your premises and remove the contents thereof for sale by Public Auction.

ROLFE (*mumbling*) And then throw dice for my garments.

FIRST BAILIFF. I beg your pardon?

SECOND BAILIFF. 'Scuse me asking, but are you by any chance a clergyman or anything of that sort? I mean—Fr Rolfe—it looks a bit like Father Rolfe. See what I mean?

ROLFE. My name is Frederick Rolfe. I have never taken Holy Orders. Had I done so, no doubt I should have been a bishop by now—not a mere priest.

SECOND BAILIFF (*guffawing good-naturedly*) Ho, ho, sir. Very good.

FIRST BAILIFF. Well, I think if you're quite clear as to the nature of our call, sir, we . . .

ROLFE. You leave me in no doubt as to the nature of your call.

FIRST BAILIFF (*producing a slip of paper*) In that case perhaps you'd be good enough to sign this undertaking not to remove your furniture or effects or any part thereof from the premises until further notice.

ROLFE. You're asking me to sign this document?

FIRST BAILIFF. That's right, sir. Just here.

ROLFE. I'm sorry, but that's something I never do.

FIRST BAILIFF. What's that, sir?

ROLFE. Sign documents. I never sign documents.

FIRST BAILIFF. Purely a formality, sir, I assure you.

ROLFE. You can assure me till the Day of Judgment, as many others have done before. Invariably their assurances were pervervid, perfidious, casuistic and, in a word, false. Ergo, no signature. Sorry.

FIRST BAILIFF. Are you saying you are refusing to sign, sir?

ROLFE. I am saying in the simplest possible language that I do not intend to sign that document. Are you satisfied?

First Bailiff. No, sir, I am not. If you refuse to sign this B sixty-three form here, I shall have no alternative but to apply immediately to the Court for a Warrant of Execution.

(*The* Second Bailiff *rises and they both move upstage*)

You've not heard the last of this, I'm afraid, sir.

Second Bailiff. Good-day, sir.

(*The* Bailiffs *exit. Alone,* Rolfe's *flippant demeanour suddenly changes to that of savage rage. He tears off his collar and tie*)

Rolfe (*through clenched teeth*) Someone will have to suffer for this.

(Mrs Crowe *appears at the door*)

Mrs Crowe. Are you by any chance speaking to me?

Rolfe (*quickly pulling himself together*) If I had heard your knock, Mrs Crowe, I would have given myself the pleasure of addressing you, but since I did not . . . (*He sits in the armchair*)

Mrs Crowe. Perhaps you would be good enough to tell me who your callers were, Mr Rolfe.

Rolfe. I'm not aware that it is part of our contract that I have to identify my visitors.

Mrs Crowe. You're in trouble again, aren't you? Were they the police?

Rolfe. No.

Mrs Crowe (*moving downstage a pace*) Well, why wouldn't they give their names, then? Is it money? (*After a pause*) It is, isn't it?

Rolfe. How can it be anything else? Of course it's money.

Mrs Crowe. So they were bailiffs then?

(*There is a silence while* Mrs Crowe *vacillates between her outraged feelings as a landlady and her concupiscent inclinations as a woman*)

(*Moving above his chair; in a wheedling voice*) Why don't you let me help you? I could help you—if you wanted me to. (*She leans over him*) You know I have always wanted to be your friend. Couldn't I be now? Mr Crowe left me quite confortable. You know that. (*She puts her hand on his arm*)

(*In loathing at her touch* Rolfe *jumps up, and in doing so kicks over the ink bottle on the floor in front of him. He hurries to wipe up the mess*)

(*Furious at the rejection of her advances*) There! (*Moving* c) Now look what you've done! Ink all over the floor! How do you suppose I'll ever get that out? It'll probably go right through the ceiling below.

Rolfe (*picking up the bottle*) I will naturally make good any damage done. (*He moves down* R)

Mrs Crowe. Make good any damage! With the bailiffs hardly
out of the house? (*Working herself up*) I'm not fooled by your high-
falutin talk any more. Before you do any more of your "making
good" you'll kindly pay me the quarter's rent you owe. Yes, and
you'll kindly pay it by the end of the week as well or I shall be
obliged to give you notice to leave. As a matter of fact, I need the
room for a business gentleman.

Rolfe. A business *gentleman?* Is there such a thing?

Mrs Crowe. An old friend of yours.

Rolfe. I haven't the slightest idea what you're talking about,
neither have I any desire to . . . Who is this person?

Mrs Crowe. Oh, I fancy you'll remember him all right. Don't
you remember Belfast?

Rolfe. Sant!

Mrs Crowe. That's right, Mr Rolfe. Mr Jeremiah Sant.

Rolfe. That Glengall Street gurrier!

Mrs Crowe. I want the room.

Rolfe (*moving below her to* l; *nervously, more to himself than to her*)
What does he want to come here for, tooting his Orange flute?
What street corner is he going to bang his Lambeg drum on this
time?

Mrs Crowe. It's none of your business. I've said what I have
to say. It's pay up or get out.

(Mrs Crowe *exits, deliberately not slamming the door*)

Rolfe (*shouting in a paroxysm of rage at the closed door*) You can't
get manure from a wooden rocking-horse, you rapacious, concupiscent—female. (*After a short pause he has second thoughts, runs to the
door, opens it, and shouts*) Mrs Crowe!

(*There is no answer*)

Mrs. Crowe, I know you're listening. When you're sorry for what
you've said, don't be afraid to say so, Mrs Crowe. (*He closes the
door and puts the blanket round his shoulders*) Someone will have to suffer
for this. (*He rolls and lights a cigarette, holding it cupped in his two
hands for warmth*) All those curves and protruberances—breeding,
that's all they're good for. (*He sits*) Jeremiah Sant is a gerry-
mandering gouger!

(*After a moment he hears footsteps on the stairs again. He listens,
wondering if it is Mrs Crowe coming back to apologize. Instead, a
letter is thrust under the door. He rises, looks at it suspiciously, then
picks it up and turns it over, looking at the seal*)

What—what's that? Archbishop's House? (*He tears the letter open
and reads it with trembling hands. Savagely*) Hell and damnation!
Imbeciles! Owl-like Hierarchs! Degenerates! (*After a pause*) God,
if ever You loved me, hear me. They have denied me the priesthood again. Not a chance do You give me, God—ever. Listen!

How can I serve You—(*to the crucifix*)—while You keep me so
sequestered? I'm intelligent. So, O God, You made me. But
intelligence must be active, potent, and perforce I am impotent and
inactive always; futile in my loneliness. Why, O God, have You
made me strange, uncommon, such a mystery to my fellow-creatures?
Am I such a ruffian as to merit total exile from them? You have
made me denuded of the power of love—to love anybody or be
loved. I shall always be detached and apart from the others. I
suppose I must go on like that to the end (*grimly*) because they are
frightened of me—frightened of the labels I put on them. (*He puts
out his cigarette savagely*) Oh God, forgive me smoking. I quite
forgot. I am not doing well at present. They force me into it: a
pose of haughty genius, subtle, learned, inaccessible. Oh, it's
wrong, wrong altogether, but what can I do? God, tell me clearly,
unmistakably and distinctly, tell me, tell me what I must do—
and make me do it. (*He sits*) Oh Lord, I am sick—and very tired.
(*His mind is in a ferment and he cannot rest*)

(*There is a knock on the door*)

(*Fiercely*) Who is it? (*He rises and moves to* L *of the door*)

AGNES (*off*) It's only me, sir.
ROLFE (*gently*) Oh! All right. Come in, Agnes.

(AGNES, *an elderly charlady, enters, wearing working clothes and an
overall. She carries a tray on which is a bowl of bread-and-milk and a
newspaper*)

AGNES. I brought you a little bread-and-milk. Whatever have
you been saying to the Missus? Oh, well, never mind. Here you
are. Eat it up whilst it's hot.
ROLFE. Thank you, Agnes. Please leave it. (*He turns away* L)
AGNES (*putting the tray on the chest*) My word, isn't it chilly in
here? Why ever haven't you turned on the . . . (*She takes a quick
look at Rolfe, sees that he is not paying attention, fumbles for her purse,
moves down* R *and, taking out a coin, puts it in the meter*)
ROLFE (*turning and seeing her*) Agnes, I forbid you . . .
AGNES (*taking matches from her apron and lighting the fire*) Get along!
Who d'you think you're forbidding then?
ROLFE (*moving over to warm himself*) You're a dear good soul,
Agnes, but you shouldn't have done that.
AGNES. You can give it me back before I go to Mass Sunday.
ROLFE. But Agnes . . .
AGNES. I know you writing folk. I've had some in my time.
ROLFE. I'm trying to tell you, Agnes, that I may not be able to
pay you back on Sunday.
AGNES. Sunday? I'm sure I never said *next* Sunday. (*Moving to
the door*) Wait till the number comes up with your name on it and
you can stand me a treat.

ROLFE (*moving to the chest*) So I will, Agnes, my word on it. (*He picks up the tray, takes it to his chair, sits, and starts to eat hungrily*)

AGNES. I don't know why you don't go back to your painting. You had ever such a lovely touch with that.

(ROLFE *is still guzzling up the bread-and-milk when his eyes fall on the newspaper. He picks it up and starts reading it, perfunctorily at first, then with ever-increasing interest*)

All those saints large as life. Some of them larger, I wouldn't be surprised. (*She begins to dust the mantelpiece then the chest*)

ROLFE. The Pope's dead.

AGNES (*not really listening*) Then there was your photography. I'm sure you could make a bit out of that—but you haven't got your camera now, have you?

ROLFE. Agnes, the Pope is dead.

AGNES. Yes, I know. God rest his soul. The poor old gentleman.

ROLFE (*reading from the paper*) " A Conclave of the Sacred College is to be convened immediately in order to elect a successor to the Holy See."

AGNES. Perhaps they'll choose our own Archbishop this time.

ROLFE (*continuing to read*) "In accordance with the Council of Lateran, the votes of two-thirds of the Cardinals present at the Conclave will be required for the election of the Supreme Pontiff. A Vatican expert reports, however, that with the present alignment among the various factions in the Sacred College, it is by no means easy to see how a clear two-thirds majority can be achieved. He goes on to suggest . . ."

AGNES. It's about time they had an English Pope for a change.

(ROLFE *turns to stare at her*)

There—I've finished you now, Mr Rolfe. See you tomorrow, then.

(AGNES *exits. ROLFE stares after her for a brief moment. Then he rises, replaces the tray on the chest, takes a fat-looking reference book from the mantelpiece and looks something up in the index. He sits, takes up his paper and pencil and starts to write rapidly with occasional reference to the book*)

ROLFE (*writing and thinking aloud*) Seven-seventy-one to seven-nincty-five, Hadrian the First. Eight-sixty-seven to eight-seventy-two, Hadrian the Second. Eight-eighty-four to eight-eighty-five—not very long, that one—Hadrian the Third. Ah—here we are. Eleven-fifty-four to eleven-fifty-nine, Nicholas Breakspeare, Hadrian the Fourth, the first and only English Pope. Ha! Son of a monk! (*He flips through the reference book again*) Hadrian the Fifth, a Genoese. Hadrian the Sixth, that's right, from Utrecht. (*He goes on working with great concentration*) In mind he was tired, worn out by years of hope deferred, of loneliness, of unrewarded toil. In body he was almost prostrate . . .

(There is a change in the lighting to a warmer hue. After a few moments, Rolfe is interrupted by a knock at the door)

Who is it?

(Mrs Crowe opens the door)

Mrs Crowe. There are two gentlemen downstairs to see you. They're clergymen.

Rolfe. Clergymen. Come in, Mrs Crowe.

(Mrs Crowe enters the room)

What sort of clergymen?

Mrs Crowe. I couldn't really say. One's an elderly gentleman, all in red and black. The other is much younger with bits of purple.

Rolfe. His Grace the Archbishop of Pimlico, and the Bishop of Caerleon—of course.

Mrs Crowe *(more intrigued than ever)* Oh. You were expecting them then?

Rolfe. They are not entirely unexpected. Now perhaps you would be good enough to . . .

Mrs Crowe. Yes, I'll bring them up.

(Mrs Crowe exits. Rolfe rushes to pick up his tie and collar and puts them on in front of the mirror. This done, he quickle adopts a dignified posture to receive his visitors. After a pause Mrs Crowe shows in Dr Courtleigh and Dr Talacryn)

This way, gentlemen. I'm sorry for all the stairs. Oh dear, I'm quite out of breath myself.

Rolfe. *Thank* you, Mrs Crowe.

Mrs Crowe. I just wondered if your guests would like some tea . . .

Rolfe. Not for the moment, thank you.

Mrs Crowe. Very well.

(Mrs Crowe exits. Courtleigh moves down c, Talacryn down lc)

Talacryn. Your Eminence, may I present Mr Rolfe . . .

(Rolfe ignores Courtleigh, goes straight to Talacryn, kneels to him and kisses the Episcopal ring on his hand. He then returns r)

Rolfe *(to Courtleigh)* Your Eminence will understand that I do not wish to be disrespectful, but the Bishop of Caerleon calls himself my friend.

Courtleigh. I hope, Mr Rolfe, that you will accept my blessing as well as Dr Talacryn's.

(Rolfe kneels and kisses the Cardinalatial ring)

ROLFE. Please sit down—as best you may.

(COURTLEIGH *sits* C. TALACRYN *stands* L *of him*)

TALACRYN. Freddy, His Eminence wishes to ask you a few questions and he thought you would not take it amiss if I were present—as your friend.

(ROLFE *acknowledges Talacryn's remark and turns to Courtleigh*)

COURTLEIGH. Mr Rolfe, it has recently been brought to my remembrance that you were at one time a candidate for Holy Orders. I am aware of all the—ah—unpleasantness which attended that portion of your career; but it is only lately that I have fully realized that you yourself have never accepted or acquiesced in, the verdict of your superiors.

ROLFE. I never have accepted it. I have never acquiesced in it. I never will accept it. I never will acquiesce in it.

COURTLEIGH. Quite, er . . .

ROLFE. But I nourish no grudge and seek no revenge. No, nor even justice. I am content to lead my own life, avoiding all my brother Catholics when circumstances throw them—

(COURTLEIGH *gets restive*)

—in my path. I don't squash cockroaches.

COURTLEIGH. And the effect upon your soul?

ROLFE. The effect upon my soul is perfectly ghastly. I have lost faith in man, and I have lost the power of loving. I have become a rudderless derelict.

COURTLEIGH. How terrible!

ROLFE. Terrible? Yes, it is indeed terrible. And, as head of the Roman Communion in this country, let the blame be upon you for the destruction of this soul.

(COURTLEIGH *raises his hands in protest*)

As for your myrmidons, I spit upon them and defy them and you may rest assured that I shall continue to fight them as long as I can hold a pen.

COURTLEIGH. Would you mind telling me your reasons?

ROLFE. I should have to say very disagreeable things, Eminence.

COURTLEIGH. Tell me the truth.

ROLFE. The Catholic and Apostolic Church, with its championing of learning and beauty, was always to me a real and living thing. It was with the highest hopes, therefore, that I entered Oscott College to begin my career as a Clerk in Holy Orders. I was soon obliged to leave, however, after a dispute with the Principal, who seemed to see no offence in grubs grazing on the lettuces and caterpillars cantering across the refectory table. The Archbishop of Agneda then invited me, on recommendation, to attend St Andrew's College at Rome. I gladly went, on the assurance that my expenses would be borne by the Archbishop. They never were and, in consequence, I was several hundred pounds out of pocket.

Courtleigh. Dear me! (*He looks at Talacryn for confirmation*)

(Talacryn *nods agreement*)

Yes?

Rolfe. Then after four months in College, I was expelled suddenly and brutally.

Courtleigh. And what reason was given?

Rolfe. No reason was ever given. The gossip of my fellow-students—immature cubs prone to acne and versed in dog Latin— was that I had no Vocation.

Courtleigh. I see. Go on.

Rolfe. Then there was the occasion in Wales when the machinations of a certain cleric, whose cloven hoof defiled the shrine of the Blessed Saint Winefred of Holywell, defrauded me of my rightful deserts for two years of arduous work undertaken at his request. Having been robbed by the said priest not only of my means of livelihood, but also of health, comfort, friends and reputation, and brought physically to my knees, he then gave me the *coup de grace* by debarring me from the Sacraments. I then had no option but to leave Wales and start life from scratch. (*Crossing below the others to* L) I walked to London. Two hundred and fourteen miles. It took me eighteen days.

Courtleigh. Good gracious! But did no one come forward to assist you at this time?

Rolfe. The Bishop of Caerleon, who somewhat belatedly received me back into Communion; one other Catholic, a man of my own trade, who later betrayed me, so I'll say no more of him; women, of course, I neglect. Eventually, others, moved no doubt by the last twitchings of their dying consciences, made tentative overtures. To these I quoted St Matthew twenty-five, verses forty-one to forty-three.

Courtleigh. Now, how does that go? (*He feels in the air with his hand for the quotation*)

Rolfe. From "I was hungered and ye gave me no meat" down to "Depart from me ye cursed, into aeonial fire".

Courtleigh. You are hard, Mr Rolfe, very hard.

Rolfe. I am what you and your fellow Catholics have made me.

Courtleigh. Poor child—poor child.

Rolfe. I request your Eminence will not speak to me in that tone. I disdain your pity at this date. The catastrophe is complete.

Courtleigh. My son, have you never caught yourself thinking kindly of your former friends? You cannot always be in a state of white-hot rage, you know.

Rolfe. Yes, Eminence, there are some with whom, strange to say, I would wish to be reconciled—when my anger is not dynamic, that is. (*He smiles*) But they do not come to me—as you have come.

COURTLEIGH. They probably do not wish to expose themselves to—ah—quotations from St Matthew's gospel.

ROLFE. Did I heave china-ware at your Lordship?

TALACRYN. You did not. (*To Courtleigh*) Your Eminence, I believe I understand Mr Rolfe's frame of mind. A burned child dreads the fire.

COURTLEIGH. True. And what course did you embark on then, Mr Rolfe?

ROLFE. I determined to occupy my energies with some pursuit for which my nature fitted me, until the Divine Giver of my Vocation should deign to manifest it to others as well as myself. I took to painting and writing. I began to write simply because, by this time, I had an imperious necessity to say certain things. (*He sits in the chair* L) In any case, ultimate penury denied me access to painting materials. So literature is now the only outlet you Catholics have left me—and believe me, I have very much to say.

COURTLEIGH. Well, well!

ROLFE. My Lord Cardinal, I do not know what you want of me, nor why you have come.

COURTLEIGH. I wished first of all to know if you still remained Catholic.

ROLFE. If I still remained Catholic!

COURTLEIGH. People who have been denied the priesthood have been known to commit apostasy.

ROLFE. Rest assured, Eminence, I am not in revolt against the Faith, but against the Faithful.

COURTLEIGH (*trying not to get angry*) I am trying to determine whether or not, at the time of which we are speaking, you formed any opinion of your own concerning your Vocation, Mr Rolfe.

ROLFE. No.

COURTLEIGH. No?

ROLFE. No. My opinion concerning my Vocation for the priesthood had been formed when I was a boy of fifteen. I have never relinquished my Divine Gift.

COURTLEIGH. You persist?

ROLFE. Your Eminence, I am not a bog-trotting Fenian or one of your Sauchiehall Street hydbrids—but English and sure; born under Cancer. Naturally I persist.

COURTLEIGH. But the man to whom Divine Providence vouchsafes a Vocation is bound to pursue it. *You* are practising as an author.

ROLFE. This is only a means to an end. (*Rising*) When I shall have earned enough to pay my debts, I shall go straight to Rome and fix the profligate priest who sacked me.

COURTLEIGH (*throwing up his hands*) Ssh!

TALACRYN (*quickly*) Your Eminence mustn't be offended by Mr Rolfe's satirical turn of phrase. He is not the man to smite those who have done him ill.

ROLFE. Do not deceive yourself, my Lord. So long as we recruit our spiritual pastors from the hooligan class, I shall smite them with all my strength.

COURTLEIGH. Really, Mr Rolfe!

TALACRYN. You're a little beside the point, Freddy.

ROLFE. Under the circumstances, His Eminence will indulge me. I've had enough of being buffeted by bishops. Until I'm the possessor of a cheque-book I do not propose to start commerce with the clergy again.

(*There is a pause while* COURTLEIGH *looks into space and* TALACRYN *looks at his toes*)

COURTLEIGH. Frederick William Rolfe, I summon you to offer yourself to me.

ROLFE (*after a pause; quietly*) I am not ready to offer myself to Your Eminence.

COURTLEIGH. Not ready?

ROLFE. I hoped I had made it clear that, in regard to my Vocation, I am marking time until I shall have earned enough to pay my debts which were so monstrously incurred on me.

COURTLEIGH. You keep harping on that string.

ROLFE. It is the only string you have left unbroken on my lute.

COURTLEIGH. Well, well; the money question need not trouble you.

ROLFE. But it does trouble me. And your amazing summons troubles me as well. Why do you come to me after all these years?

COURTLEIGH. It is precisely because of these years—how many was it?

ROLFE. Call it twenty.

COURTLEIGH—that we must take your singular persistency as proof of the genuineness of your Vocation. And therefore, I am here today to summon you to accept Holy Orders with no delay beyond the canonical intervals.

ROLFE. In two years' time, when I shall have published three more books, I will respond to your summons. Not till then.

TALACRYN. But His Eminence has said that the money question need not hinder you.

ROLFE. Yes, and the Archbishop of Agneda said the same.

(COURTLEIGH *looks as if he is going to explode, and* TALACRYN *hastens to intervene*)

TALACRYN. I am witness of His Eminence's words, Freddy.

ROLFE. What's the good of that? Supposing in a couple of months His Eminence chooses to alter his mind? Could I hail a prince of the church before a secular tribunal? Would I? Could I subpoena Your Lordship to testify against your Metropolitan and Provincial? (*Crossing below to down* R) Could I? Would I? Would you?

(COURTLEIGH *makes as if to interject, but* ROLFE *cuts in*)

My Lord Cardinal, I must speak, and you must hear me. You are offering me the Priesthood on good and legitimate grounds, for which I thank God. But, if I correctly interpret you, you are also offering me something in the shape of money, and I will be no man's pensioner.

COURTLEIGH (*mildly*) Please understand me, Mr Rolfe, that the monies in question are being offered solely as restitution for the years in which you were denied the Priesthood.

ROLFE. Oh! (*After a pause*) No, I will not take charity.

TALACRYN. Well, then, Freddy, in what form will you accept this act of justice from us? Do make an effort to believe we are sincerely in earnest and that in this matter we are in your hands. (*Turning to Courtleigh*) I may say that, Your Eminence?

COURTLEIGH. Unreservedly.

(*There is a pause while* ROLFE *considers*)

ROLFE (*quietly but with determination*) I will accept a written expression of regret for the wrongs which have been done to me by both Your Eminence and by others who have followed your advice, command or example.

COURTLEIGH (*taking a folded piece of paper from his breviary*) It is here.

ROLFE (*at first surprised, then reading it with care*) I thank Your Eminence. (*He tears the paper into pieces*)

COURTLEIGH. Man alive!

ROLFE. I do not care to preserve a record of my superiors' humiliation.

COURTLEIGH (*with an effort*) I see that Mr Rolfe knows how to behave nobly, Frank.

ROLFE. Only now and again. But I had long ago arranged to do just that.

(*The prelates make a gesture of incomprehension to each other.* COURT-LEIGH *stands.* ROLFE *kneels and receives benedictions*)

COURTLEIGH. We shall see you then at Archbishop's House tomorrow morning, Mr Rolfe.

ROLFE. I will be there at half-past seven to confess to the Bishop of Caerleon. Your Eminence says Mass at eight and will give me to Holy Communion. Then, if it please Your Eminence, you will give me the four Minor Orders. In the meantime, I will go and have a Turkish bath and buy myself a Roman collar.

(COURTLEIGH *moves to the door.* ROLFE *goes quickly up and opens it.* COURTLEIGH *exits.* TALACRYN *is about to follow*)

Your Lordship doesn't happen to know the price of collars these days?

TALACRYN (*apologetically*) I haven't the slightest idea, I'm afraid.

Rolfe. Well then, just to be on the safe side, perhaps you wouldn't mind springing me a fiver.

Talacryn (*embarrassed*) Oh, certainly. Certainly (*He fumbles in his pockets for his wallet. Eventually he finds it and gives a banknote to Rolfe*) Thank you.

Rolfe (*graciously*) Not at all. See you tomorrow.

(Talacryn *exits, leaving the door open.* Rolfe *goes to the mirror, takes off his tie and turns his collar back to front. He then gives his reflection an episcopal blessing. Suddenly he freezes. He sees a reflection of somebody behind him. He turns round to see* Jeremiah Sant *standing in the doorway*)

Sant!

Sant. Still at your play-acting, I see! What part is it this time?

Rolfe. What are you doing in here?

Sant. I've come to look at my room.

Rolfe. *Your* room?

Sant. Aye. I've been given to understand that you've got your marching orders again.

Rolfe. What do you mean?

Sant (*moving down* c) The Order of the Boot. You're out. Just like old times, isn't it?

Rolfe (*changing tactics*) Yes, as a matter of fact I do have to leave here as it happens. I've been summoned for work elsewhere.

Sant. Summoned, have ye? Summonsed, more likely, from what I know of you.

Rolfe (*crossing* l) Meanwhile this room is mine until the end of the week.

Sant. Aye, if you've paid the rent.

Rolfe. Get out of here.

Sant. Oh, aye, I'm going, but I'll be back on Saturday, so make sure you're away by then.

Rolfe. Why do you persist in hounding me in this way? What did I ever do to you?

Sant. I'll tell you a wee story. You'll mind Belfast down by the docks where the shipyard workers live.

Rolfe (*sitting down* l) It is not a memory I particularly cherish.

Sant. Aye, likely not. (*He pauses for the painful memory to sink in*) Well, we lived in one of those streets when I was a young feller. The houses were all painted the same colours—green and brown in good oil paint because those were the colours of the line they were building in the shipyard at the time.

Rolfe. I'm not particularly interested in the social anthropology of Belfast.

Sant. Maybe, but I'll tell ye all the same. Ours was a Protestant street, you see, and on a blank wall at the end of it was a life-size portrait of King Billy—William of Orange riding into battle on a white charger—against the Popeheads.

ROLFE. That was Cargill Street, and one of your wittier co-religionists had also painted "Kick the Pope" on a gable-end.

SANT. I'm coming to who kicks who in a minute. The next street to ours was a Catholic street . . .

ROLFE. Paintwork by courtesy of the Cunard Steamship Company.

SANT. Let me finish. One day my wee brother Sam—he was only eleven years old at the time—wandered down that street. God knows why he did, but he did. He got into a fight. Some elder boys joined in. Those Papishes got him down on the ground and they kicked him. They went on kicking him till he stopped moving.

ROLFE. I heard.

SANT. Aye, they left him for dead. But he wasn't—not quite. Whenever I'm back in Belfast I go and see him at the asylum. He was thirty-two last birthday, but he's still only eleven in his mind. Just lately he's taken to wetting his bed again.

ROLFE. Tragic. But one act of hooliganism begets another.

SANT. That may be what you call it. But the Lord saith, an eye for an eye and a tooth for a tooth—and I'm still biding my time. (*He moves to the door*) When you go, leave the window wide, will ye. It's the smell of a Papish I can't abide.

(SANT *exists, leaving the door open, and singing as he goes* "*The sash my father wore*")

> "Our Father knew the Rome of old
> And evil is thy fame.
> Thy kind embrace the galling chain,
> Thy kiss the blazing flame."

ROLFE *rises and stands quite still for a moment. His triumphant mood has vanished and, once more, he looks trapped and hunted. After a moment's thought he springs into action. Pulling a holdall out from the corner up* C *he puts it on the chair, takes a few effects from the chest of drawers and throws them in, then goes to the door and listens to make sure the coast is clear. Having satisfied himself on this count he picks up the holdall and tiptoes out, as the* LIGHTS *fade to a*

BLACKOUT

SCENE 2

SCENE.—*A room in Archbishop House. Seven-thirty the following morning. The only furniture is an upright armchair set* C *and facing at an angle up* LC, *and a thick cushion set close* L *of the chair.*

As the LIGHTS *come up,* TALACRYN *enters from an opening up* R *and moves to the chair. A moment later* ROLFE *enters up* L.

TALACRYN. Good morning, Freddy. I hope your new lodgings are comfortable.

ROLFE. Compared to Broadhurst Gardens, they are as the Elysian Fields.

TALACRYN. I never cared much for N.W. 6 either. (*He sits in the chair, facing up* LC) Now—shall we get this over?

ROLFE. It may take rather a long time.

TALACRYN. All day if necessary. (*He takes a small violet stole which he has been carrying on his arm, kisses the cross embroidered on it, and puts it round his shoulders. He then sits in the chair, facing up* LC)

(ROLFE *kneels on the cushion facing downstage, so that he has a three-quarter back view of the Bishop. He makes the sign of the cross. Both skip through the ritual beginning and end of the confession pretty fast*)

ROLFE. Bless me, Father, for I have sinned.

TALACRYN. May the Lord be in thine heart and on thy lips, that thou with truth and humility mayest confess thy sins, (*he makes the sign of the cross*) in the name of the Father and of the Son and of the Holy Ghost, Amen.

ROLFE. I last confessed five days ago.

TALACRYN. Since then, my son?

ROLFE. Since then I broke the first commandment by being superstitiously silly enough to come downstairs in my socks because I had accidentally put on my left shoe before my right. I broke the third commandment by permitting my mind to be distracted by the palpably Dublin accent of the Priest who said Mass on Saturday.

TALACRYN. Is there any more on your conscience, my son?

ROLFE. Lots. I confess that I have broken the sixth commandment by continuing to read an epigram in the Anthology after I had found out that it was obscene. I have broken the third commandment of the Church by eating dripping toast for tea on Friday. I was hungry; it was very nice. I made a good meal of it and couldn't eat any dinner. This was thoughtless at first, then wilful.

TALACRYN. Are you bound to fast this Lent?

ROLFE. Yes, Father. I should now like to make a general confession of the chief sins of my life.

TALACRYN. Proceed, my son.

ROLFE. I earnestly desire to do God's will in all things, but I often fail. I like to worship my Maker alone, unseen of all save him. That is why I cannot hear Mass with devotion in those churches where one is obliged to squat in a pew like a Protestant, with other people's hot and filthy breath blowing down my neck. My mind has a twist towards frivolity, towards perversity. I have been irreverent and disobedient to my superiors. For example, I said that the legs of a certain domestic prelate were formed like little Jacobean communion-rails.

(TALACRYN *reacts slightly to this last*)

I have told improper stories—not of the revolting kind, but those which are witty, anti-protestant or recondite—the sort common among the clergy. Being anti-pathetic to fish, I once made an enemy sick by the filthy comparison which I used in regard to some oysters which he was about to eat. I confess that two or three times in my life I have delighted in impure thoughts inspired by some lines in Cicero's *Oration for Marcus Coelius.*

TALACRYN. I don't for the moment recall—well, never mind. Is there anything further?

ROLFE. There is one thing which I have never mentioned in confession except in vague terms only.

TALACRYN. Relieve your mind, my son.

ROLFE. Father, I confess I have not kept my senses in proper custody. Sometimes I catch myself extracting elements of aesthetic enjoyment from unaesthetic situations.

TALACRYN. Can you be more precise, my son?

ROLFE. Yes, Well, for example, I once was present at the amputation of a leg. Under anaesthetics, directly the saw touched the marrow of the thigh bone, the other leg began to kick. I was next to it, and the surgeon told me to hold it still. It was ghastly, but I did. And then I actually caught myself admiring the exquisite silky texture of the human skin. Father, I am a very sorry Christian. I confess all these sins, all the sins which I cannot remember, all the sins of my life. I implore pardon of God; and from thee, O Father, penance and absolution. (*Quickly*) Therefore, I beseech blessed Mary Ever-Virgin, Blessed Michael Archangel, Blessed John Baptist, the Holy Apostles, Peter and Paul, all saints and thee, O Father, to pray for me to the Lord our God.

TALACRYN. My son, do you love God?

(*From silence, tardily the response emerges*)

ROLFE. I don't know. I really don't know. He is the Maker of the World to me. He is Truth and Righteousness and Beauty. He is first. He is last. He is Lord of all to me. I absolutely believe in Him. I unconditionally trust Him. I am ready and willing to make any kind of sacrifice for Him. So far I clearly see. Then in my mind, there comes a great gap—filled with fog.

TALACRYN. Do you love your neighbour?

ROLFE. What? Who?

TALACRYN. Do you love your neighbour?

ROLFE. No. Frankly, I detest him—and her. Most people are repulsive to me, because they are ugly in person, or in manner, or in mind. I have met those with whom I should like to be in sympathy, but I have been unable to get near enough to them.

TALACRYN. Could you not love them?

ROLFE. No.

TALACRYN. Do you love yourself?

ROLFE. On the whole, I think I despise myself, body, mind and soul. I do look after my body and cultivate my mind. And naturally I stick up for myself, but—no, my body and mind are no particular pleasure to me.

TALACRYN. Have you anything else to confess, my son?

ROLFE. Nothing. Really nothing, Father. I'm very tired. I long to be at rest.

TALACRYN. That is actually the longing of your soul for God. Cultivate that longing, my son, for it will lead you to love Him. Thank Him with all your heart for this great gift of longing. At the same time remember the words of Christ our Saviour: "If ye Love Me, keep My Commandments." Remember, He definitely commands you to love your neighbour. Serve the servants of God, and you will learn to love God. You have tasted the pleasures of this world and they are as ashes in your mouth. In the tremendous dignity to which you have been called—the dignity of the priest-hood, you will be subject to fiercer temptations than those which have assaulted you in the past. Brace the great natural strength of your will to resist them. Begin to love your neighbour so that you may soon consciously come to love God. My son, the key to all your difficulties, past, present and to come, is love. For your penance, you will say—no, the penance for minor orders is rather long—for your penance you will say the Divine Praises with the celebrant after Mass. And now say after me:

(*The ritual is gabbled through,* ROLFE *repeating quickly after* TALACRYN)

O my God, most worthy of all love—I grieve from my heart for having sinned against Thee—And I purpose by Thy Grace—Never more to offend Thee for the time to come.

(TALACRYN *continues alone, making the sign of the cross*)

Ego te absolvo in Nomine Patris et Filii et Spiritus Sancti, Amen. Go in peace and pray for me.

(ROLFE *and* TALACRYN *rise and move downstage together.* TALACRYN *resumes his informal manner*)

But before you do, I have been instructed by His Eminence to inform you that you will accompany him to Rome tomorrow. You will act as his private chaplain at the Conclave while the new Pope is being elected. We will travel together, Freddy.

ROLFE *and* TALACRYN *move upstage towards the exit* R. *A single bell starts to toll insistently. An echoing Liturgy is distantly heard as the* LIGHTS *fade to a*

BLACKOUT

SCENE 3

SCENE—*A Chapel in the Vatican.*

As the LIGHTS *come up, a bell tolls in the distance and the Liturgy continues
to be heard in some remote side chapel. The only furnishings are two
candelabra, up* RC *and* LC. *Two* ACOLYTES *(boys) in surplices enter,
from up* R *and up* L, *genuflect in unison towards the direction of the altar,
and proceed to light the candelabra with long tapers. Having done so, they
genuflect again, and both exit up* R. TALACRYN *and* ROLFE *enter
together up* L. *Their hands are folded, clasping breviaries.* ROLFE, *now
in Holy Orders, wears a black soutane and biretta.* TALACRYN *wears
similar garb suitable to a bishop. As they speak the following dialogue,
they perambulate round the stage together.*

ROLFE (*sniffing at the smell of incense*) Nothing stinks like the odour
of sanctity.

TALACRYN. Now, now.

ROLFE (*pointing out front*) Look at those frescos. Wasn't it Mark
Twain who said: "The Creator made Italy from designs by
Michelangelo"?

TALACRYN (*distrait*) Very possibly. Their Eminences are still
sitting, it seems.

ROLFE. On two addled eggs apiece.

TALACRYN. Freddy, I beg you—the whole world is waiting for
the imminent announcement of a new Pope, and you make jokes
in rather doubtful taste.

ROLFE. Let me assure Your Lordship that my flippancy in no
way reflects my concern with the outcome of the Sacred Consistory.
I've studied the form of those members of the Sacred College who
could be said to be possible starters for the Supreme Pontificate,
and it's my belief that the short-odds favourite . . .

TALACRYN. Short-odds favourite!

ROLFE. A sporting metaphor, indicating . . .

TALACRYN. I am acquainted with the jargon of the Turf, Freddy.

ROLFE. Then if I may continue the analogy, it's perfectly plain
to a student of form that the short-odds favourite must be the
present Secretary of State, Cardinal Ragna, whom God preserve.

TALACRYN. Not everyone would say "Amen" to that, I fear.

ROLFE. But then there is the malpractice called "Bumping and
Boring"—

TALACRYN—much frowned upon by the stewards—

ROLFE—and I very much doubt whether Cardinal Ragna will
be allowed to trot away with the race. Our own Archbishop, for
example, would nominate the Parish Priest of Ballyjamesduff if it
would keep Ragna out.

TALACRYN. Steady.

ROLFE. And I'm prepared to bet a thousand pound to a penny-halfpenny stamp that the Conclave has broken down again for the simple reason that Ragna's been nobbled.

TALACRYN (*smiling*) I wish I had it in me to be quite so irreverent as you, Freddy.

ROLFE. Perhaps, but I doubt if Your Lordship has it in him to be quite so devout either. You are a natural Christian, my Lord Bishop. I, on the other hand, am a religious maniac.

TALACRYN. You do yourself an injustice.

ROLFE (*casually*) I know I do. (*Looking up at a fresco on the ceiling*) Isn't that superb? (*Pointing*) Look at that. A little lacking in generosity in describing—(*he makes a graphic gesture*)—but compared to a figure like that, what can people see to admire in the female form?

TALACRYN. It's a matter of taste, I suppose.

ROLFE (*looking at Talacryn*) What a waste!

TALACRYN. What is a waste?

ROLFE. That such a fine, upstanding man as Your Lordship should have felt inclined to accept the celibacy of priesthood.

TALACRYN. Good heavens, Freddy, If you are being serious, I can assure you that from the moment I took Orders no other thought ever occurred to me.

ROLFE. Nevertheless one has to admit that the vestigial nipples on a man are about as useful as the Pontifical pudenda. Had I been a Renaissance Pope, I should have insisted that . . .

(*A bell begins to clang insistently*)

Something seems to be happening.

(ROLFE *moves down* L. TALACRYN *follows to* R *of him*)

TALACRYN. I think they must have risen.

ROLFE. Who?

TALACRYN. The Cardinal-Compromissaries.

ROLFE. Will they have reached a decision?

TALACRYN. We shall soon see. Here they come.

(*The nine* CARDINAL-COMPROMISSARIES, *in full purple, led by the* CARDINAL ARCHDEACON, *and in company with thurifers and cross-bearers, appear from the rear of the auditorium and move in procession down the aisles to the stage, chanting the Christus Vincit as they move. Arriving on the stage, they form an arc from* R *to above* TALACRYN LC. *The* CARDINAL-ARCHDEACON *remains extreme* R. *Lastly comes an* ACOLYTE *bearing the Papal Crown—the Triple Tiara—on a cushion.* ALL *bow in the direction of the altar, then turn inwards. As soon as everyone is in position the bell ceases*)

ROLFE (*in a whisper to Talacryn*) What is it? What is happening?

TALACRYN. I think God has given us a Pope.

ROLFE. Whom?

(*The Litany ceases, and* ALL *turn to face Rolfe and Talacryn. All except Rolfe kneel*)

CARDINAL ARCHDEACON. Reverend Lord, the Sacred College has elected thee to be the successor to St Peter. Wilt thou accept pontificality?

(*Since all present are now facing towards Rolfe and Talacryn,* ROLFE *assumes it is the latter who is being addressed. He turns towards Talacryn with a happy smile.* TALACRYN, *however, is kneeling. Confused,* ROLFE *turns back to look at the Cardinal Archdeacon*)

(*with greater emphasis*) Reverend Lord, the Sacred College has elected thee to be the successor to St Peter. Wilt thou accept pontificality?

(*There is another pause.* ROLFE, *looking round to where all are on their knees facing inwards towards him, at last realizes that the awful question is addressed to him*)

ROLFE. *Reverend* Lord? Will *I*?

TALACRYN (*in a whisper*) The response is *Volo*—or *Nolo*.

(ROLFE *takes a deep breath, crossing his right hand over his left on his breast*)

ROLFE. *Volo*—I will.

An organ peals out, as—

the CURTAIN *falls*

ACT II

SCENE 1

SCENE—*Mrs Crowe's parlour in London.*
  *There is a chaise-longue set below a screen at an angle from C to down
  LC, with a small table at the head of it. On the table is a bottle of
  whiskey. No other furnishing is necessary.*

When the CURTAIN *rises,* MRS CROWE *is seated upstage on the
chaise-longue, with* JEREMIAH SANT *beside her. Both have drinks in
their hands.* SANT *is a member of the FRS—Fellowship of Religious
Segregation, an extremist group, outlawed in Ulster, dedicated to the
persecution of Roman Catholics in general and the Pope in particular. He
is a draper by profession and a street corner rabble-rousing politician who
does not stop at violence. A dangerous fanatic. He is reading aloud
from a newspaper.*

SANT. Here, listen to this—" . . . and as representatives of the
Catholic world looked on, the triple crown was placed on the head
of the first English Pope to ascend the throne of St Peter since
Nicholas Breakspeare became Pope Hadrian the Fourth in eleven
fifty-four." (*He interrupts himself*) Begod, doesn't it make you want
to puke to think of an Englishman sinking so low.
MRS CROWE. What's so special about it, Jerry? I can't see why
you get so excited about it.
SANT. Get so excited about it? (*Rising and moving* L) Rome rule
means Home Rule, doesn't it? But I'm thinking maybe the
Papishes have cooked their own goose this time.
MRS CROWE. How's that then?
SANT. Well, for one thing, it will queer the pitch of the Home
Rulers. One false move and it could be civil war in Ireland with
the Fenians cutting each other's dirty throats. They'll not stand
for an Englishman giving out of orders, Pope or no.
MRS CROWE. Oh, I'll never understand Irish politics as long as
I live. Here, let me fill your glass.
SANT. Aye. You do that, sweetheart.

  (*There is a pause.* SANT *has now blown off most of his steam.* MRS
  CROWE *fills both glasses*)

MRS CROWE. Looking after men—that's something I do understand.
SANT. True for you, Nancy. (*He sits beside her*) Never a truer
word. Slainte!
MRS CROWE. Here's cheers.

SANT. But there's one thing I've never been able to find out—
what you see in that abomination of desolation.

MRS CROWE. Who?

SANT. Rolfe.

MRS CROWE. What *I* see in *him*? Oh, please, Jerry. Give me a
little credit. Do you know what he used to do? No, I don't want
to talk about it. I can't bear to speak about him any more. (*She
starts to snivel*)

SANT. Now just a moment, Nancy. Just a moment. (*He rises and
moves below the chaise-longue to R of the table and picks up the bottle*)
Here, give us your glass.

MRS CROWE (*upset*) Oh, no thank you, Jerry.

SANT. Come on, sweetheart. Just a half'un.

MRS CROWE. Oh, all right then.

(SANT *fills both glasses and sits again. They drink.* MRS CROWE
makes a face)

Oooh, this is strong. (*She downs it in one, nevertheless*)

SANT. Never mind. It'll do you good. Now, Nance, just now
you started to say something and bye-and-bye you're going to
finish it. But first I'm going to tell you one or two things.

MRS CROWE. What things?

SANT. Well, first, how would you like to come on a wee trip
with me to Rome?

MRS CROWE. To Rome? But, Jerry, how could I? I mean . . .

SANT. Oh, don't you worry about that. We'll be properly
chaperoned, I promise you.

MRS CROWE. But I've got nothing to wear.

SANT. No problem at all. (*He rises and moves R*) Now just listen
to me. The Fellowship of Religious Segregation, of which, as you
may know, I'm a Senior Brother, are very disturbed by certain
recent events and, as loyal servants of the Crown, we feel it our duty
to do whatever we can to protect the Free Churches of the United
Kingdom. (*He postures about the room*)

MRS CROWE. Yes, Jerry, but what's this all to do with you and
me going to Rome?

SANT. I'll tell ye in a minute. Now the FRS are sending a
deputation to the Vatican to demand certain safeguards for Pro-
testants in the light of the aforesaid recent events, and I'm heading
the deputation. " Sing and rejoice, O daughter of Zion: for, lo,
I come, and I will dwell in the midst of thee, saith the Lord."

MRS CROWE (*impressed*) Oh, I say.

SANT. Now, you'll be asking yourself—and rightly—why I'm
inviting you to come with me, and I wouldn't insult your intelligence
by trying to pretend that it was just for business reasons only—
here, where's your glass? (*He fills the two glasses again*)

MRS CROWE (*holding out her glass*) Not another. (*She accepts
without further demur*)

Sant. Besides, I think I can say, Nance, that we know one another too well for that.

Mrs Crowe. Oh, it is nice to see you back again, Jerry, I must say. Things have not been too easy for me lately, one way and another.

Sant. Aye, I suspected as much when I came. And I wouldn't be surprised if it were something to do with that agent of the Whore of Babylon, the erstwhile Baron Corvo. Eh?

(Mrs Crowe *does not reply, but consoles herself with another drink*)

I'm right, Nancy, aren't I?

(Mrs Crowe *nods her head*)

That little barmstick! And I'll wager he hasn't paid you the rent —sneaking out of the house the way he did.

Mrs Crowe (*getting maudlin*) And not even a line to say he'd got there safely—not even a postcard. (*She starts to snivel*)

Sant. Aye. Well, we'll soon get even with him. (*He moves back to his seat beside her, and puts his arm round her shoulders*) Now a little earlier you were going to tell me something. Now's the time. Come on, Nance.

Mrs Crowe. No, I couldn't, Jerry. (*She snivels*)

Sant (*getting tough*) Now, Nancy, you can and you shall tell me.

Mrs Crowe (*content that the moment has come to give in*) Oh, Jerry, it's been going on for years. He—he wouldn't leave me alone, never. He was always—always trying to—to do things to me, even when Mr Crowe was alive. I've had no peace whenever he was around, Jerry, and I—I just couldn't keep him away. (*She turns and buries her head in Sant's shoulder, sobbing*)

Sant (*surprised*) Well I'll be damned!

Mrs Crowe. Well, don't sound so surprised. Aren't I attractive any more?

Sant. No, no. Of course you are, sweetheart. It's just that I always thought . . . Anyway, no Papish traitor shall defile with his dirty touch a respectable Protestant lady and get away with it. He shall pay right dearly for this or my name's not Jeremiah Sant.

Mrs Crowe (*quietly and viciously*) Make him squirm, Jerry. Make him squirm.

Sant *kisses her violently on the mouth as the* Lights *fade to a—*

BLACKOUT

SCENE 2

Scene—*An Audience Chamber in the Vatican.*
The only furniture is the Pontifical Throne, which is set c, *on a small dais.*

As the Lights *come up,* Cardinal Ragna, *Secretary of State, an elderly, bull-like Italian,* Cardinal Berstein, *a cold, arrogant German and* Father St Albans, *Propositor-General of Jesuits, the truculent "Black Pope", an Englishman, enter together from up* r *and move down* c. Ragna *is* c, *with* Berstein *to* r *and* St Albans *to* l *of him.*

St Albans. To a great extent I blame myself. I should have known what a formidable politician my compatriot, Cardinal Courtleigh, was. When it became apparent that (*inclining towards Ragna*) Your Lordship's candidature was being blocked by the French and Iberian faction—

(Ragna *makes a gesture of disgust*)

—you should have pressed for old Gentilotto.

Berstein. Gentilotto would have been good. An old man but a good man. He would have been no trouble.

St Albans. I had no idea that he had in mind this *parvenu.*

Ragna. *Parvenu, si.*

St Albans. Still less that he could have succeeded in foisting him on all nine of you.

Berstein. We must search afresh, he said. We must search outside the Vatican, he said, for a man of Faith and Constancy, a man of Simplicity and Humility, he said. Huh! Humility.

St Albans. He had the humility of an Old Testament prophet.

(*During the following, all three turn and walk slowly upstage and back*)

Ragna. And you saw also the business of the Pontifical ring! Why must he insist to have an amethyst ring? The late Holiness take always the emerald ring. But no—the ceremony of Consecration is delayed one half-hour to find amethyst ring. Who does he think he is, this man?

St Albans. I think he thinks he's Pope—with some justification, of course.

Ragna (*disgustedly*) Eh! "He who was a frog, is now a king."

Berstein. "He who is born of a hen always scratches the ground."

Ragna. *Si. E vero!* And when the Cardinal Archdeacon say, "Holiness, what is the Pontifical name you will choose?", he say, "Hadrian the Seventh". I said to him—you heard me, no? "Your Holiness would perhaps prefer to be called Leo, or Pius, or Gregory, as is the modern manner." But he say—

St Albans (*imitating Rolfe*)—"The first and previous English Pontiff was Hadrian the Fourth; the second and present English

Pontiff is Hadrian the Seventh. It pleases Us; and so, by Our Own impulse, We command."

Ragna (*in disgust*) "By Our Own impulse We command." Such arrogance! Eh! But you heard what he said to me when I tell him it is very *pericoloso*—

St Albans—dangerous—

Ragne—dangerous to walk to Lateran?

St Albans. My Lord Berstein and I were somewhat distant from Your Lordship at the time.

Ragna. I said for the Holy Father to walk in Lateran through streets of Rome today is madness. The city is full of Jews and Freemasons. "It is suicide for you," I say, "and is murder for me."

St Albans. And what did he say?

Ragna. He say, "Good, the Church is badly wanting a new martyr", (*He strides down* L)

(St Albans *and* Berstein *also move* L, St Albans *suppressing laughter*, Berstein *tut-tutting*. Courtleigh, Talacryn *and other members of the Sacred College enter up* R. Courtleigh *is wheeled on in a bathchair, to down* RC. Talacryn *also moves* RC. *The others form a semicircle on either side of the Throne, which remains vacant*)

Courtleigh. Can anyone enlighten me as to the reason for this hasty summons?

Ragna (*with a gesture of resignation*) *Ecco*!

Courtleigh. Had to gobble me breakfast. Haven't even had a moment to read *The Times*.

St Albans. Your Eminence could hardly have done so.

Courtleigh. What do you mean?

St Albans. I am informed that an embargo has been placed on all newspapers within the Vatican.

Courtleigh. Extraordinary!

St Albans. However, I made it my business to find out the reason for this, and it appears that the embargo was placed by His Holiness prior to the publication of his Bull and Breve.

(*There are exclamations of astonishment from several Cardinals*)

Further, I made it my business to obtain a copy of the text of this Bull and Breve and I think Your Eminence's will be interested if I read it to you.

(*More exclamations*. St Albans *clears his throat and pauses for effect. He then reads from a sheet of paper. The* Cardinals *stop muttering*)

" We, Hadrian the Seventh, Vicar of Christ, Servant of the servants of God, speak thus: We find Ourselves the sovereign of an estate to which We hold no title deeds. But Our Kingdom is not of this world. So, therefore, We, Vicar of Christ, Successor to the Throne of St Peter, do now make Our formal and unconditional renunciation to temporal Sovereignty."

(*The* Cardinals *gasp*)

"Our predecessors followed other counsels and they acted in the knowledge of their responsibility to God. We, on Our part, act as We deem best. We are God's Vice-regent and this is Our will. (*Quickly*) Given at Rome, at St Peter's by the Vatican, on this day of Our Supreme Pontificate."

(*There is a moment of utter silence*)

Ragna (*shouting*) Judas! Judas! This shall not be!

St Albans. Unfortunately, Lord Cardinal, it can be—and is.

Ragna. Am I Secretary of State or am I not Secretary of State? I am asking Your Eminences. If the Pontiff is no longer temporal sovereign, how am I Secretary of the Vatican State? You tell me I am to be dismissed by this—this clerk who has the sack from two —not one, but two—ecclesiastical colleges?

Berstein. Two colleges! (*He tut-tuts*)

Talacryn. His Holiness believes the world is sick for want of the Church. He believes, I think, that we should turn all our efforts and attention to the pursuit of non-secular matters.

Ragna (*striding* r *and back to* l) *Va bene, va bene.* But I tell you His Holiness has very special conception of His Apostolic character. He think that is enough. It is not enough.

Berstein. Ja, ja. It is not enough. If the temporal power is worth having, it is worth fighting for.

St Albans. I do not say that I disagree with Your Eminence.

Ragna. Then perhaps you will make a suggestion. You say Jesuits are always very clever. Why do you not suggest we convene the Oecumenical Council? Eh?

Berstein. Ja, ja. The Oecumenical Council only can deal with such matters.

Ragna. I say this man is a heretic. I say he is the Anti-Pope. And I say the Sacred College must act now—before it is too late.

St Albans. And I wouldn't necessarily argue with Your Eminence, but the Oecumenical Council of the Vatican has stood adjourned since—I think I am right in saying—since eighteen-seventy. All the same . . .

Ragna. But all the same it can be reconvened, no?

Berstein. Under the circumstances it is the only thing to do. I agree.

St Albans. If the Sacred College should choose to demand . . .

Ragna (*roaring*) The Sacred College *should* demand

(*Unnoticed,* Hadrian (Rolfe) *enters quietly from up* r. *For the first time he is seen wearing the white garments of a Pope. He carries a large leather folder*)

If there's any anxiety or doubt in any minds the Sacred College *must* demand.

HADRIAN (*moving* R *of the throne; very quietly*) Pray, what must the Sacred College demand, Lord Cardinal?

(*All react to the sudden appearance of the Pope.* RAGNA, *taken off guard, can only work his jaw defiantly.* HADRIAN *persists in his most ominously gentle voice*)

Your Eminence is free to address Us.

RAGNA (*recovering his truculence slightly*) I wish rather to address the Sacred College.

HADRIAN (*sweetly*) You have Our permission to do so. (*He looks round the room, noting the reactions of those present*)

RAGNA (*moving* L *of the throne*) I wish to—(*He clears his throat to gain time*) I wish to . . .

HADRIAN. You wish to denounce Us as Heretic and Pseudo-pontiff. And to do so, you wish to convene an Oecumenical Council. Is that not correct?

(RAGNA, *his own words taken from his mouth, remains silent, his face working*)

That generally is done by oblique-eyed cardinals who cannot accustom themselves to new pontiffs. (*Mounting the dais*) But Lord Cardinals, if such an idea should be presented to you, be ye mindful that none but the Supreme Pontiff can convoke an Oecumenical Council, and that the decrees of such are ineffective without the express sanction of the Supreme Pontiff. We are conscious of your love and of your loathing for Our Person and Our Acts. We value the one and regret the other. But ye voluntarily have sworn obedience to Us, and We claim it. Nothing must and nothing shall obstruct Us. Let that be known. (*He sits on the throne*) Wherefore Most Eminent Lords and Venerable Fathers, let not the sheep of Christ's flock be neglected while the shepherds exchange anathemas. Try, Venerable Fathers, to believe that the time has come for taking stock. Ask yourselves whether we really are as successful as we think we are—whether in fact we are not abject and lament-able failures in the eyes of God. We have added and added to the riches, pomp and power of the Church, yet everywhere there is great wealth alongside dire poverty; there are strong nations brutally holding small ones to slavery; above all there are millions of people of goodwill looking to us for moral and spiritual leadership who get from us only dogmatic interpretations of Canon Law in return. If, then, we have so far failed in spreading Christ's Gospel, let us try anew. Let us try the road of Apostolic simplicity—the simplicity of Peter the Fisherman. At least let us try.

(*There is total silence*)

Your Eminences have permission to retire.

(*For a moment there is silence. Then* TALACRYN *goes quickly to re-affirm his allegiance by kissing the Pontifical ring. Hesitantly at first,*

the others follow. RAGNA, *still recalcitrant, makes the briefest possible
acknowledgement.* COURTLEIGH *alone is left, in his chair. Having made
obeisance, the prelates move off up* R, *murmuring*)

BERSTEIN (*as he goes, muttering*) His Holiness has averted a schism.

HADRIAN (*to Courtleigh*) We should be glad if Your Eminence
could spare a few moments longer of your time.

COURTLEIGH (*cooly*) I am at Your Holiness's disposal. I pray
Your Holiness will forgive this chair.

HADRIAN. We trust Your Eminence is not seriously incommoded.

COURTLEIGH. A very English complaint, Holy Father, a touch
of the gout.

HADRIAN. Accept Our sympathy for your English complaint. We
too have them, but of a different nature. We desire to establish
relations with Your Eminence, chiefly because you hold so re-
sponsible a position in England, a country dear above all others
to Us.

COURTLEIGH (*putting on his Cardinalatial Mask expressive of the old
and wise condescending to give ear to the young and rash*) Proceed, Most
Holy Father.

HADRIAN. It is Our wish to make England's people prepared
for the Lord. But we find Ourselves impeded at the outset by the
present conduct of the English Roman Catholics—especially of the
aboriginal English Catholics.

(COURTLEIGH *reacts sharply, then bows slightly and continues to
attend.* HADRIAN *opens his folder, which contain press cuttings*)

Kindly give Us your opinion of this statement, Eminence. I quote
from a London newspaper whose views are not necessarily our own.
"The Roman Catholic laity resident in England are asking Parlia-
ment to set up some control over Roman Catholic monies and
interests. It is alleged that no account is afforded by the Roman
Catholic Bishops of the management or disbursement of such
properties and monies." Well?

COURTLEIGH. The scandal emanated from a priest of my Arch-
diocese, Holiness. We were successful in preventing it from spreading.

HADRIAN. Oh! Then there was such a petition? I was prepared
to ascribe it to the imagination of one of the bright young men
usually employed by the monstrous old proprietor of this newspaper.
And were there many supporters of the petition?

COURTLEIGH (*raising a hand*) Unfortunately, there were a number.

HADRIAN. And were there any grounds for the allegations?

COURTLEIGH. Holy Father, we cannot be expected to account
to every Tom, Dick and Harry for the hundreds of bequests and
endowments which we administer.

HADRIAN. Why not, if your accounts are properly audited? We
assume they are?

COURTLEIGH. Ah—to a great extent, yes.

HADRIAN. To a great extent? Not invariably? But do you really consider your clergy capable of financial administration?

COURTLEIGH. As capable, as other men.

HADRIAN. Priests are not "as other men".

COURTLEIGH. But what would Your Holiness have?

HADRIAN. We entirely disapprove of the clergy using any secular power whatever, especially such power as inheres in the command of money. The clergy are ministers—ministers—not masters. The clergy are *more*, not *less* human, and they certainly are not the pick of humanity.

COURTLEIGH. Even if I were to agree, I still do not precisely see Your Holiness's point.

HADRIAN. No? Then let us take another. (*He rises and moves* LC, *taking a small green ticket from the folder*) This comes from Your Eminence's diocese. "Church of the Sacred Heart—admit bearer to Midnight Mass—Christmas Eve—Middle Seat one shilling and sixpence." Surely not some form of discrimination?

COURTLEIGH (*shrugging, as if the card were of no significance*) A small attempt to prevent—ah—improper persons from attending these services.

HADRIAN. But "improper" persons should be encouraged to attend.

COURTLEIGH (*irritated*) And have scenes of disorder and pro-anation?

HADRIAN. We are determined that Our Churches be made as free to the lost as to the saved.

COURTLEIGH. May I be permitted to ask what experience Your Holiness has had in parochial administration?

HADRIAN. You could answer that question yourself, Your Eminence. But I've attended many midnight masses and heard no sign of the profanation of which you speak. Sots and harlots were undoubtedly present, but they were not disorderly. They were cowed, they were sleepy, they were curious, but they made no noise. If means of grace are obtainable in a church, who dare deny them to those who need them most? You are here to serve—and only to serve. We especially disapprove of any system which makes access to the church difficult—like this admission fee.

COURTLEIGH. Holy Father, the clergy must live.

HADRIAN. And so they shall. But pew-rents are abominable—and so are pews. Abolish them both.

COURTLEIGH (*beside himself with rage*) Your Holiness speaks as though He was not one of us.

(HADRIAN *pauses and fixes Courtleigh with a look*)

HADRIAN.   Look at your Catholic Directory and see the advertisement of a priest who is prepared to pay bank interest on investments—in plain words, to be a money-lender in direct contravention to St Luke. Look at the Catholic Hour and see the advertisement of a priest who actually trades as a tobacconist. Look in the precincts of your churches and see the tables of the Fenian literature sellers and the seats of them that sell tickets for stage plays and bazaars. No, my Lord Cardinal, the clergy attempt too much. They may be excellent priests, but as tradesmen, stock jobbers and variety entertainers, they are catastrophes.

COURTLEIGH (*with resignation*) But Holy Father, do think for a moment. What are the clergy to live on?

HADRIAN. The free-will offerings of the faithful.

COURTLEIGH. But suppose the faithful do not give of their free-will?

HADRIAN. Then starve and go to heaven.

COURTLEIGH (*stung once more to defend himself*) Your Holiness will permit me to remind you that I, myself, was consecrated Bishop fourteen years before you were made a Christian at baptism. It seems to me that you should give your seniors credit for having consciences of their own.

HADRIAN (*circling slowly below Courtleigh's chair, above it, behind the throne, and L of it to C*) My dear Lord Cardinal, if We had seen the least sign of the said consciences . . .

COURTLEIGH. I am not the only member of the Sacred College who thinks that Your Holiness's attitude partakes of—shall I say singularity—and—ah—arrogance.

HADRIAN. Singularity? Oh, We sincerely hope so. But arrogance —We cannot call it arrogance that We have attempted to show you something of Our frame of mind.

COURTLEIGH. What, then, Holy Father, would You wish me to do?

HADRIAN. We wish you to act upon the sum of Our words and conduct in order that England may have a good, and not a bad, example from English Catholics. No more than that. The Barque of Peter is way off course. Lord Cardinal, can the new captain count on the loyal support of His Lieutenant in trying to bring her head round?

COURTLEIGH (*making an immense effort*) Holy Father, I assure you that You may count on me.

HADRIAN. We realize the immense effort on your part that has made you give Us this assurance and it gladdens Us to see this evidence of the Grace of your Divine Vocation.

(COURTLEIGH *bows slightly*)

Well now, Lord Cardinal, to change the metaphor, let us put away the flail and take up the crook. So shall we take a little stroll in the garden and say some Office?

COURTLEIGH (*surprised*) Oh, well, certainly, with pleasure—that is if Your Holiness doesn't mind walking by the side of my bathchair, that is . . .

HADRIAN. Oh, but We do. It is Our invariable custom to walk *behind* bathchairs and push them.

COURTLEIGH. Oh but, Holiness, I could not for one moment permit . . .

HADRIAN. No, but for just one hour you will submit.

COURTLEIGH. But, Holy Father, really . . .

HADRIAN (*putting his folder on Courtleigh's lap and moving behind the bathchair*) Nonsense man, do you suppose that One has never pushed a bathchair before?

COURTLEIGH. All the same, Holiness, it is hardly . . .

HADRIAN. Now sit quietly and open your breviary and start reading the office.

(COURTLEIGH *obeys*)

We will look over your shoulder and make the responses. (*He swivels the bathchair round*) It's awfully good exercise, you know.

Respectively saying and responding to the Office of the Day, HADRIAN *pushes the aged* COURTLEIGH *slowly off up* R, *as the* LIGHTS *fade to a—*

BLACKOUT

SCENE 3

SCENE—*Outside a cafe in Rome.*
    A table and two chairs are set down L.

When the LIGHTS *come up,* SANT *and* MRS CROWE *are sitting at the table, which is outside the café.* MRS CROWE, *seated* L, *is shielding herself with a parasol.* SANT, R, *fans himself with a Panama hat. He holds a piece of paper in his other hand.*

SANT. This is my ultimatum. Listen. (*He reads*) " Since my earlier communication in which I had the pleasure of addressing you on the aims of the Fellowship of Religious Segregation, I have been anxiously waiting the favour of an acknowledgement of same. In case the subject has slipped your memory, I should remind you that we were not adverse to give our careful consideration to any proposal you may see fit to make, financial or otherwise." That's putting it fair and square, eh?

MRS CROWE. Yes, Jerry, but how's he going to know that you want to talk to him about the other—you know . . .

SANT. Hold your horses. I haven't come to the guts of it yet. (*Continuing to read*) "But I am quite at a loss to understand on what grounds you have not yet favoured me with a reply unless there is anything on which you would like further explanation. In which case, I will be most happy to call on you per appointment for which I have been waiting at the above address here in Rome for some weeks and neglecting my business at considerable expense and inconvenience which a man in my position cannot be expected to incur and common courtesy demands should be made good."

The LIGHTS *fade to a—*

BLACKOUT

SCENE 4

Scene—*The Audience Chamber.*

As the Lights *come up,* Talacryn *and* Hadrian *are entering up* R. Talacryn *is reading the remainder of Sant's letter.* Hadrian *is smoking a home-rolled cigarette. He moves to the throne and sits still and tense as Talacryn reads*)

Talacryn ". . . I therefore trust that in view of the not altogether pleasant facts that are in the possession of myself and another party well known to yourself, you will see fit to accord me a private interview at your earliest convenience. Hoping that I will not . . ."

(Hadrian *remains rigid. His hand trembles as he removes his cigarette*)

Hadrian. Stop! I cannot bring myself to hear any more of that illiterate filth.

Talacryn. Forgive the presumption, but Your Holiness seems unduly upset by this impertinent nonsense.

Hadrian. It is not His Holiness who is upset, but Frederick William Rolfe.

Talacryn. Again forgive the presumption, but one has known Your Holiness for some years. Who are these enemies, Holy Father?

Hadrian. Prurient scum. Pithycanthropoids and Neanderthals who beset Our path in Our previous and ghastly existence. Worms who turn to traduce Us.

Talacryn. They can be annihilated, Holiness. Surely some guillotine can be brought down that would effectively silence these —these . . .

Hadrian. Blackmailers? Since Our conscience is clear, We have no desire to be so dynamic. We should not touch ordure even with a shovel.

Talacryn. But silence is more likely to inflame such people than to quiet them. Supposing in their frustration they go to the newspapers?

Hadrian. Then, doubtless, the Sacred College will erect their tail feathers and gobble like a flock of huge turkey-cocks: "Behold the Anti-Pope!" they will say, and glare whole Inquisitions at us.

Talacryn. Respectfully, Holiness, the matter should not be allowed to reach such a pass. As Your Holiness rightly assumes, those within the Sacred College who were against Your accession would welcome a scandal directed at Your Person.

Hadrian. Let them have a scandal. Let them keep aloof in their vermillion sulks. It is not Our will to move in this matter.

Talacryn. But, forgive me if I persist, Holiness . . .

Hadrian (*sharply*) Do not persist. (*He rises and moves* LC, *putting out his cigarette with his foot. Changing from the pontifical to the familiar*) Tell me, Frank, what have you been doing today?

TALACRYN. Today? Oh, I paid a visit, as a matter of fact, to Your old college.

HADRIAN (*freezing*) Oh?

TALACRYN. They cannot understand why You have not yet been to see them.

HADRIAN. Is not the Rector still the same man who once expelled me—brutally and without explanation?

TALACRYN. The Rector is an old man now, sensible to the errors of his youth, as we all are.

HADRIAN (*to himself*) The wound goes deep. It has never properly healed.

TALACRYN. Perhaps this is the moment for cauterizing the wound, Holiness. Strangely, I forgot the horrors of my own times there after I'd visited them once or twice. Besides, the young men love to see one, and the older men—the principals—like to see vermilion take note of them.

HADRIAN (*suddenly moving to Talacryn*) Frank, let's go to the College now. We can get there in time for lunch?

TALACRYN (*looking pleased*) What a good idea.

As TALACRYN *and* HADRIAN *move quickly upstage, the* LIGHTS *fade to a—*

BLACKOUT

SCENE 5

SCENE—*The College.*
The stage is bare.

As the LIGHTS *come up we hear a distant bell, and a distant Litany being chanted. Some young* SEMINARISTS *in purple Sopranos pass across from up* R *to up* L, *singing. Among them is* ROSE. *When they have passed from sight,* HADRIAN *enters* R *with* TALACRYN *and the* RECTOR. *The* RECTOR, *dressed in black, is an old man whose behaviour before the Pope is a mixture of self-importance and obsequiousness—the Headmaster humouring a distinguished parent. The three men move* C, *the* RECTOR *between* HADRIAN, L *and* TALACRYN, R.

RECTOR. This has been a great day for the College, Holy Father.

(HADRIAN *ignores the flattery*)

Of course, had we known Your holiness intended to honour us, a proper reception . . .

HADRIAN. Quite unnecessary. Our children expect to see Us and We came to be seen. We now wish to know something of one student in particular.

RECTOR. Who is that, Holy Father?

HADRIAN. The somewhat older man who looks so hungry and took only bread and water at luncheon.

RECTOR. Ah, poor fellow!

HADRIAN. Now why do you say that, Monsignore?

RECTOR. Well, Holiness, I'm afraid this is not the place for him. He's very sensitive and doesn't really get on with the others.

HADRIAN. Does he quarrel with them?

RECTOR. Oh no. But he takes pains to avoid them.

HADRIAN. Perhaps he has his reasons.

RECTOR. Perhaps, but his attitude does not seem suitable in one hoping to attain Orders! He is not what I would call a good mixer.

HADRIAN. You talk as if he aspired to be a sporting parson.

RECTOR (*nettled*) I must tell Your Holiness that I do not feel that he has a real Vocation for the priesthood.

HADRIAN. Please know, Monsignore, that We have not come here to brag or to gloat, but we feel bound to remind you that your judgment as to vocation has, in the past, been in error.

RECTOR (*shaken*) I am only too mindful—Your Holiness's personal case has for a long time been—it was a long time ago. I can only say in extenuation that to err is human.

HADRIAN (*crossing below the others to* R) Human error is sometimes excusable. *In*human behaviour is not. Ill-considered judgments by those in authority are damnably culpable.

(*The* RECTOR *winces*)

What is the name of this student who has "no vocation"?

RECTOR. Rose, Holiness. George Arthur Rose.

HADRIAN. We wish to speak to him.

RECTOR. If it pleases Your Holiness.

HADRIAN. We will speak to him alone.

(*The* RECTOR *bows and exits up* R)

(*To Talacryn, when they are alone*) Were We too severe, Frank? The wish to smoke has made Us irritable.

TALACRYN (*smiling*) Your holiness was altogether admirable. I must admit to having enjoyed the last five minutes more than a Christian should.

(*During the following speeches* HADRIAN *and* TALACRYN *stroll up and down* L)

HADRIAN (*looking round and sniffing*) Still the same smell; boiled mutton-fat and hot boy.

TALACRYN. They seem to be the inescapable adjuncts of education.

HADRIAN. Inescapable? Nonsense! We have half a mind to appoint you Protector of this College. Yes, that's right. A Celtic Protector for a Celtic College. Good. We shall give you a breve as soon as We get back to the Vatican. You will give them sanitation —and sanity, for goodness sake. You might make that shrubbery into a gymnasium. And what about a swimming pool—with a lovely terrace on the top?

TALACRYN. I don't see why not.

HADRIAN. And, Frank, make friends with them and see what you can do to take that horrible secretive suppressed look out of their young eyes. You understand?

TALACRYN. I think so, Holiness.

(*The* RECTOR *enters up* R *with* ROSE, *who is dressed in the violet cassock and black soprano of a seminarist*)

RECTOR. Mr Rose, Your Holiness.

(ROSE *observes the forms, and moves to* C)

HADRIAN. You will be pleased to hear, Monsignore, that We have appointed Cardinal Talacryn Protector of St Andrew's College. His Eminence would be most grateful if you would now take him on a detailed tour of the kitchens and sanitary arrangements.

(*The* RECTOR *looks surprised, but is now totally submissive*)

RECTOR. As Your Holiness pleases.

(*The* RECTOR *and* TALACRYN *exit up* R. ROSE *does not show surprise but stands up* C *throughout with dignity and reserve*)

HADRIAN (*moving* R *of Rose*) Dear son, on slight knowledge We have the impression you are one of the unhappy ones. Will you confide in Us?

ROSE. Sanctity, I have not complained.

HADRIAN. But now you may do so.

ROSE. I have no reason—I do not wish to do so.

HADRIAN. How old are you, my son?

ROSE. Sanctity, twenty-nine.

HADRIAN. And you find your environment disagreeable?

ROSE. All environments are more or less disagreeable to me.

HADRIAN. Up to the present at least. You find that your circumstances adversely influence your conduct—prevent you from doing yourself justice—here.

ROSE. That may be my fault.

HADRIAN. They mock you, no doubt.

ROSE. I suppose that is the case, Holiness.

HADRIAN. So was Jesus Christ mocked. But why are you?

ROSE. Because for my ablutions I carry two cans of water up two-hundred and two steps every day.

HADRIAN. No doubt they say you must be a very unclean person to need so much washing.

ROSE. Sanctity, you are quoting the Rector. How does Your Holiness know so exactly?

HADRIAN (*laughing*) Have they even put a snake in your water cans?

ROSE. No, they have not done that.

HADRIAN. They did in Ours. Isn't it absurd?

ROSE. It is—and very disconcerting.

HADRIAN. But you try not to let it disconcert you?

ROSE. I try but I fail. My heart is always on my sleeve and the daws peck it. So I try to protect myself in isolation.

HADRIAN. That they call "sulkiness"!

ROSE. Yes, Your Holiness knows so exactly . . .

HADRIAN (*moving slowly upstage; almost to himself*) We also were never able to arrange to be loved. (*He circles slowly above Rose and down to* LC) Do you always live on bread and water?

ROSE. Yes, except for eggs.

HADRIAN. Why?

ROSE. I have been into the kitchen and seen—things. They cannot deposit sputum inside the shells of boiled eggs.

HADRIAN (*moving across the stage to down* R) Do you like bread and water?

ROSE. No, but in order not to be singular I eat and drink what I can of what is set before me. But because of that, I am deemed more singular than ever.

HADRIAN (*moving round above Rose to* LC *as before*) Yet you choose to persevere, my son!

ROSE. Sanctity, I must. I am called.

HADRIAN. You are sure of that?

ROSE. It is the only thing in all the world of which I am sure.

HADRIAN. Yet you know that this college is not the place for you?

ROSE. A suppose not. But my diocesan sent me here and I intend to serve my sentence.

HADRIAN. Dear son, what is your ambition?

ROSE. Priesthood.

HADRIAN. And you *will* persevere—for however long?

ROSE. For twenty years if need be.

HADRIAN. We persevered for just that length of time.

ROSE. Then so will I.

HADRIAN. My son, it is in Our power to grant you a favour. Do you wish to ask Us for anything?

ROSE. No thank you, Sanctity.

HADRIAN. My son, do you think you are ready for priesthood?

ROSE. I am ready as soon as I may be summoned, Sanctity.

HADRIAN. You shall be summoned. Come to Vatican tomorrow and ask for Cardinal Talacryn. He will expect you. Your desire may soon be fulfilled. Will you pray for Us, dear son?

ROSE. Holy Father, I most surely will.

HADRIAN. Good bye, and God bless you.

(ROSE *kneels and* HADRIAN *gives blessing.* ROSE *exits* R *and* HADRIAN *moves down* L. TALACRYN *and the* RECTOR *enter up* L. *The* RECTOR *crosses and exits up* R. TALACRYN *moves downstage to Hadrian*)

What a delicious day it has been, Frank. You persuaded Us and We are grateful.

TALACRYN. I think the walk did your Holiness good.

HADRIAN. It was not just the walk, but something quite other— as though a curtain has been lifted, or, more exactly, as if We had been given a brief glimpse into a human heart.

TALACRYN. That is a rare and wonderful experience, Holiness.

HADRIAN. Rare? You are Our confessor. You must know that for Us the experience is unique. Frank, We have just had the first feeling of undiluted enjoyment of human society which We can ever remember.

TALACRYN. Do you remember what I said to you in London, Holiness? I said that if You could find it in Yourself to love your neighbour it would lead You to love God.

HADRIAN. Love—yes—We have recognized for the first time in Ourselves a new and unborn power, a perfectly strange capability. Today, We have made experience of a feeling which—well, which We suppose—at any rate will pass for—Love.

As they move up R *the* LIGHTS *fade to a—*

BLACKOUT

SCENE 6

SCENE—*The Audience Chamber.*
A small chair has been set down RC, *facing towards the throne.*

When the LIGHTS *come up,* AGNES *is discovered sitting on the chair* RC *looking very nervous.* FATHER ROSE, *now in the cassock of an ordained priest, enters up* L. *He has a clip of papers in his hand.*

FR ROSE. Mrs Dixon?

AGNES. Yers?

FR ROSE. His Holiness asked me to convey his apologies to you. He has been slightly delayed.

AGNES. That's quite all right, dear, ta.

(FR ROSE *nods and moves* L *of the throne. There is an awkward silence as they both wait for Hadrian*)

Been keeping busy then?

FR ROSE (*slightly taken aback*) Well, as a private chaplain to His Holiness I find the days full.

AGNES. I daresay you do. He's a handful all right. When I used to look after him myself . . .

(*Further conversation is prevented by the entrance of* HADRIAN *up* L)

FR ROSE. Mrs Agnes Dixon, Your Holiness.

(AGNES *rises, trots to* C *and flops on her knees.* HADRIAN *immediately attempts to assist her to rise*)

HADRIAN. Agnes.

AGNES. Oooh, my joints!

HADRIAN (*throwing off completely his cold pontifical manner*) Agnes, please sit down.

AGNES. I don't mind, sir.

HADRIAN (*moving her chair R of the throne*) Please, Agnes, here.

AGNES (*sitting*) Oooh, that's better. I've been on my feet all day, and don't these marble floors tell.

HADRIAN (*sitting on the throne*) I'm sorry, Agnes.

AGNES. I shouldn't be saying such things, should I, not now with you living here.

HADRIAN. Good friends are few, Agnes—particularly in the Vatican.

AGNES: These your chairs, are they?

HADRIAN. Well, I suppose they go with the job.

AGNES. Not very comfy, are they? Still—oh, there I am again! But there, I can't help but think of you still as Mr Rolfe I used to do for.

HADRIAN. It's good to hear you say so, Agnes.

AGNES (*scrabbling in her capacious bag and bringing forth a packet*) Here we are, then.

HADRIAN (*taking it*) What is this?

AGNES. Why, the change, of course.

HADRIAN. Change?

AGNES. From the money you sent me to buy that house. I got it cheaper than we thought because it'd been empty so long.

HADRIAN. Oh, but you dear good soul, I didn't expect any change. It's all yours. Besides, you may need it to tide you over till you get the lodgers.

AGNES. Till I can get the lodgers? Why, I'm turning them away already.

HADRIAN. Good, well bank it for the winter. (*He returns the packet to her*) Do you remember cooking two dinners one Christmas Day? One was ate. The other you carried to some fellow who was out of work. I remember because you spilt gravy on your frock and hoped I hadn't seen.

AGNES. No-one can't say you haven't got a long memory, can they?

HADRIAN. You stinted yourself then, Agnes. Now don't stint yourself any more. Give away as many hot dinners as you please.

AGNES. Well, I'm one of the lucky ones, I reckon. It's not easy for some nowadays, particularly the old 'uns what have no family. (*She dives in her bag again*) I nearly forgot, what with all the excitement and walking along those stone corridors with those gentlemen in their fancy get-up. One of them was ever so stuck-up, he was. I couldn't help saying, "I seen plenty more like you, my lad, at the old Holborn Empire". Oh yes, I did, but I don't think he knew what I meant. There, I knew I had it somewhere. (*She produces a jar of pickles*) It's the pickles you always had a fancy for.

Made just the same as I used to. You always had a tooth for them, didn't you?

HADRIAN. Dear, good Agnes, you're kindness itself. You know, I never get anything like this nowadays. George, try one.

(*All three help themselves to a pickled onion.* FR ROSE *gallantly tries to conceal his dislike. There is a long pause as they all munch*)

AGNES (*with her mouth full*) Well, I must say its good to see you again, sir, for all you've come up in the world. All the same, I shall never get used to your being Pope, never. Oh, I hope you don't think I don't know my place!

HADRIAN (*rising*) Your place, Agnes, is always close to Our heart.

AGNES (*rising*) Well, I mustn't detain you, Mr Rolfe, so I'll be getting along just as soon as you give me a blessing and say a bit of a prayer. Thank you, sir, for all you've done and I'll say a prayer for you every day for as long as I'm spared.

(AGNES *gets, with some difficulty, to her knees and receives the Pontifical Blessing*)

HADRIAN (*causing her to rise*) Are you going back at once, Agnes?

AGNES. Well, I was thinking of having a bit of a look-round before going back. It's silly to come all this way and not see the sights.

HADRIAN (*taking a card and pen from Fr Rose*) Then take this card— (*He writes on the card*)—give it to the "fancy gentleman" who is going to take you downstairs and tell him what you want to see.

AGNES. Will they want me to give the card up at the door?

HADRIAN. Not if you want to keep it.

AGNES. I'll keep this card till I'm laid out. God bless you, my dear. (*She kisses the Pope's ring, gets up, not without difficulty, and moves up* R)

(FR ROSE *goes to* AGNES *and they both exit up* R)

HADRIAN (*moving* LC) Filthy hypocrite! (*After a pause, he smiles gently to himself*)

(TALACRYN *enters with unusual lack of formality. He obviously bears urgent news*)

TALACRYN (*moving quickly down* L *to Hadrian*) Forgive my precipitance, Holiness, but the news I bring—is of the greatest urgency.

HADRIAN (*still unconcerned*) You're quite breathless, Frank, A man of your weight must take care. (*He taps his heart significantly*)

TALACRYN. Holiness, please let me be serious. Calumnies have been published. Terrible things have been said.

HADRIAN (*freezing*) Oh? What sort of things? By whom? Who has published them?

TALACRYN. Malignant things referring to Your Holiness's secular life. Published in an Ulster newspaper, and worse . . .

HADRIAN. Yes?

TALCRYN. In a prominent journal sponsored by the Church.

HADRIAN. Who has written this? What has been said?

(RAGNA *swirls in triumphantly up* R, *bearing a sheaf of newspapers. He moves* R *of the throne. All the other* CARDINALS *follow him on and form an arc, some moving* RC, *others behind the throne to* LC)

RAGNA. Perhaps these will inform Your Holiness.

(HADRIAN *moves* L *of the throne and takes the papers*)

Your Holiness is well qualified to appreciate the validity of your English newspapers.

(HADRIAN *starts to read*)

These English newspapers have been to much trouble. Suddenly they find it very interesting to make study of the life of the English Pope. They find very interesting things.

HADRIAN (*still reading; half to himself*) Things unanswerable because the merest whisper distorts truth.

RAGNA. The English reporters are careful to begin at the beginning—His Holiness was expelled from ecclesiastical college in Roma because he is owing everybody money. He makes friends with old Italian lady, the Duchess of Sforza-Cesarini, who is very rich.

HADRIAN (*to himself*) Unanswerable, because it is half-truth.

RAGNA. Back in England, His Holiness becomes "Baron Corvo", a fine gentleman who inherited title from his noble Italian friend. He used title to gain influence and obtain more money.

HADRIAN (*still to himself*) Half-truth again. Who could have attacked with such malign ingenuity?

RAGNA. The Baron tries to buy some property, but people find he is not "Baron". He has no money to buy property. He is a fraud, an adventurer.

HADRIAN (*searching the column*) Anonymous! Anonymous half-truths. I should be able to recognize the filthy paw of this muck-raker.

RAGNA. So "Baron Corvo" runs away—to another town where he makes more trouble and owes more money; this time in Wales.

HADRIAN. We were not in Wales this time—but in Belfast. Yes, of course—Sant! Jeremiah Sant!

RAGNA. But in Ireland it is also the same story; he is again the great gentleman—the writer, photographer, inventor of many things, a friend of many famous people. But it is all lies. He has no money. He has no friends. He is nothing, He owes money to the people where he is living. They take him from bed and put him in the street. They throw his clothes after him so he must dress in the street.

(TALACRYN *reacts sharply at this humiliating revelation*)

HADRIAN (*looking at Ragna*) Yes. We appear to be a very disreputable character, do we not. But we demand, Lord Cardinal, that you take note of certain errors.

RAGNA. Errors in Your English newspapers?

HADRIAN. Ten, eleven, twelve, thirteen, fourteen, fifteen—why should English newspapers be less corrupt than Italian? Fifteen absolute and deliberate lies, in a column and a half of print. (*He returns the newspapers and sits on the throne*) Well, Lord Cardinal?

RAGNA (*getting angry*) Very well, you tell me this is all lies. But today the whole world is reading these papers. What are You going to do?

HADRIAN (*icily*) We will ponder the matter Your Eminence has set before Us, and at a convenient time We will declare Our pleasure.

RAGNA (*almost apoplectic*) Convenient time, eh? Let me remind Your Holiness that I am Cardinal Secretary of State of the Vatican, and I demand to know what you are going to do.

HADRIAN. Very well, then. (*He leaps up and significantly draws off the Pontifical ring and puts it on the seat of the throne, Then he walks down* C *and faces the Cardinals upstage. Dropping the Pontificial manner*) Gentlemen, would some of you like to put Frederick William Rolfe to the question?

(*After an embarrassed pause, there is a general murmur of assent*)

COURTLEIGH. We—that is—many of us feel that Your Holiness has been grossly misrepresented. We would appreciate a statement to refute these calumnies by the Press.

HADRIAN (*in a voice of icy reticence*) Very well. I will give to the Sacred College that statement. And when I have finished speaking I never will return to this subject.

COURTLEIGH. Then if Your Holiness would enlighten . . .

HADRIAN. There is no Holiness here.

COURTLEIGH (*bowing acknowledgement*) One confesses that the question of pseudonyms is of interest.

HADRIAN (*moving upstage to the throne and turning below it*) Pseudonyms: when I was kicked out of St Andrew's College without a farthing or a friend I was obliged to live by my wits. Thank God who gave me wits to live by. Think of this: I was a tonsured clerk forced to earn a living by secular means, but always intending to persist in my Divine Vocation. I had a shuddering repugnance from associating my name, the name by which some day I should be known in the priesthood, with secular pursuits, so I adopted a pseudonym. But as time went on and Church malfeasance drove me from one trade to another, I split up my personality and carried on each trade under a separate pseudonym: as Baron Corvo I wrote and painted and photographed; as F. Austin I designed decorations; as Frank Hockheimer I did journalism. There were four at least. Four entities careering round like colts in a meadow dissipating energy which, but for the imbecility of the Church, could have been canalized to fulfil its proper purpose years ago.

RAGNA (*tapping the newspapers*) What about the debts? Perhaps you explain the debts, please.

HADRIAN. Debts! From the moment they were first contracted with the connivance and consent of certain prelates not unknown to some of you here—

(COURTLEIGH *and* TALACRYN *show signs of embarrassment*)

—debts were never off my chest for twenty years. I was foolish enough to believe that you Catholics would keep your promises and pay me for the work which I did at your orders. So I accepted credit. I worked—God knows how I worked—and expected a just wage. When it was withheld, people encouraged me to hope and work on. They offered me the odd guinea to go on with. I took the filthy guinea. God forgive me for becoming so degraded. But one can't pay one's debts and lead a Godly life for ever on an occasional guinea. My weakness, my fault was that I did not die—murdered at St Andrew's College. (*He turns away* L)

BERSTEIN. Perhaps you will now condescend to explain the allegations of luxurious living . . .

TALACRYN (*to Hadrian*) Holy Father, don't say another word. (*Turning to his colleagues*) Shame on you. How can you torture the man so! Can't you see what you're doing, wracking the poor soul like this? Pulling him in little pieces all over again.

(*There are sounds of assent from several Cardinals*)

BERSTEIN. I think it would be in the best interest if we were to hear everything.

COURTLEIGH. Surely, My Lords, we have heard enough . . .

HADRIAN (*mounting the dais*) But you shall hear more. They say that I gorged myself with sumptuous banquets at grand hotels. Once, after several days of starvation, I got a hard-earned be-grudging and overdue fee from a magazine. I went and had an omelette at a small-town commercial doss-house which called itself "The Grand Hotel". They also say that, in my lodgings, I demanded elaborate dishes to be made from my own cookery book. Since I was beholden to my landlords I did indeed ask for special dishes— dishes of lentils and carrots—I do not touch meat—anything that was cheapest, cleanest, easiest and most filling. Each dish cost a few pence and I sometimes had one each day. And occasionally when I earned a little bit I spent a few shillings on apparatus conducive to personal cleanliness, soap, baths and so on. That is the story of my luxurious living, My Lords.

(*There is a pause, and all keep silent*)

(*Moving downstage and facing up*) I have been provoked, abused, calumniated, traduced with insinuation, innuendo, misrepresenta-tion, lies; my life has been held up to ridicule and most inferior contempt. I tell you this because, officially, I must correct an error. You may take it as an example of how your Catholics, laymen and clergy alike, can tire out and drive almost to death a man's body—perhaps even his soul (*Moving upstage and turning*) But understand this, My Lords: by no words will I ever defend myself outside these walls. Nor do I speak in my own defence, Venerable Fathers, even to you. I, personally and of predilection, am indifferent to opinions, but it is your right to hear that which you have heard.

(*There is another silence, then* RAGNA *speaks out*)

RAGNA (*waving the newspapers*) An enemy hath done this!

HADRIAN (*with candid delight*) Those are the first genuine words I have heard from Your Eminence's heart.

RAGNA (*in a voice of thunder*) Who is it has done this evil thing?

TALACRYN. A reactionary blackmailer and a disappointed woman —two worms that have turned.

RAGNA (*roaring*) *Anathema sint:* Let them be smothered in the dunghill.

(*Slowly,* HADRIAN *picks up the Pontificial ring, places it on his finger, and sits*)

HADRIAN (*in Pontifical manner*) Lord Cardinals, it is Our wish to be alone.

(*The* CARDINALS *exit up* R *and up* L. RAGNA *is the last to turn to go*)

Lord Cardinal.

RAGNA (*turning and moving* L *of the dais*) Holiness?

HADRIAN (*rising*) May we detain you a moment longer?

RAGNA. Please, Holiness.

(HADRIAN *and* RAGNA *move downstage together,* RAGNA *to* R)

HADRIAN (*with warmth and charm, in contrast to his earlier manner*) We are happy to think that Your Eminence is no longer opposed to Us.

RAGNA (*responding warmly*) I too am happy, Most Holy Father, that God has opened my eyes to the injustices done to Your Holiness. I beg that Your Holiness will forgive me for blindness in the past.

HADRIAN (*deceptively docile*) Your Eminence is already forgiven. We are particularly pleased to have your Lordship's co-operation at the present time since there is a matter particular close to Our heart on which We would welcome your advice.

(*During the following,* HADRIAN *and* RAGNA *slowly circle the stage, behind the throne and down* LC)

RAGNA. Pray open Your heart, Most Holy Father.

HADRIAN. Very well. (*No bomb was ever dropped more gently*) By way of emphasizing the essential difference between the Church Temporal which We have already renounced—and the Church Apostolic, We have in mind to give away the Vatican Treasure.

RAGNA (*shaken*) The Vatican Treasure! But has Your Holiness considered that most of the treasures are consecrated to the service of the Church?

HADRIAN. Yes. We have also considered that the Church exists for the service of God in His creatures. She does not serve either by keeping costly and beautiful things shut up in cupboards. Well, my Lord? Are you with Us or against Us?

RAGNA (*after a pause*) Holy Father, I am with You with all my heart. Under Your inspired guidance let the Church once more meet the world in the pure missionary spirit of Her greatest days. I shall follow whenever Your Holiness may lead.

HADRIAN. God bless Your Eminence for that. To tell the truth, I was in no mood for another fight.

(*They both laugh*)

Your Eminence, may I now suggest that you accompany Us to St John Lateran?

RAGNA. *Va bene*. With great pleasure, Most Holy Father.

HADRIAN. They will be saying prayers there for those having authority in the Church. It would seem to be suitable occasion to celebrate our reconciliation.

RAGNA. *Benissimo*. Will Your Holiness go by carriage or in the sedia gestatoria?

HADRIAN. Perhaps Your Eminence is in the mood to indulge Our English eccentricities even further?

RAGNA (*falling into the trap*) With pleasure, Your Holiness. Of course.

HADRIAN (*with a smile*) Then we will walk.

RAGNA (*aghast*) Walk! But, Holiness . . .

HADRIAN. Your Eminence did say you would follow wherever We may lead. (*He claps his hands*)

(FR ROSE *enters up* R)

My sunshade, George. Cardinal Ragna is walking with us to Lateran.

(FR ROSE *exits*)

RAGNA. But, Holy Father, the political situation is very, very dangerous.

(FR ROSE *enters with the white, Pontifical sunshade with its green lining.* HADRIAN *crosses and takes it from him*).

HADRIAN (*smiling*) Quite. But as We mentioned to Your Eminence once before . . .

RAGNA (*raising his hands to heaven*) But, Holiness, I am too fat to become a martyr.

HADRIAN (*opening the sunshade*) My Lord Cardinal, in every fat priest, there is always a bony martyr crying our for Beatitude.

HADRIAN *leads off up* R, *followed by the now faithful* RAGNA *crossing himself and tut-tutting, as the* LIGHTS *fade to a—*

BLACKOUT

SCENE 7

SCENE—*The same.*

Two chairs have been set RC *and* LC *facing up towards the throne.*

As the LIGHTS *come up, a body of* SWISS GUARDS *enters up* R *and take up their positions in an arc across the back of the stage. They are followed by two* CHAMBERLAINS *escorting* SANT *and* MRS CROWE *from up* L. SANT *attempts a truculent nonchalance,* MRS CROWE *is obviously nervous. The* SENIOR CHAMBERLAIN *escorts them to the chairs,* SANT *to* LC *and* MRS CROWE RC, *then both* CHAMBERLAINS *retire upstage. There is a silence in which* SANT *and* MRS CROWE *sit awkwardly facing a ring of implacable* SWITZERS.

MRS CROWE (*in a stage whisper*) Oh dear, why don't they hurry up? Oh, I do wish I'd never come.

SANT (*also in a stage whisper*) Shut up, Nancy. Do you want them to hear you?

MRS CROWE. I just wish it was all over, that's all.

SANT. Can't you see that's just what he wants? He wants to get us rattled. But I'll rattle him first. (*He clinks the loose change in his pocket*) Ay.

MRS CROWE. Oh, I do hope you're right, Jerry.

SANT. Of course I am. You don't imagine I gave the papers all I know, do you? Not by a long chalk I didn't. Not by a very long chalk. He'll listen to me this time, or my name's not Jeremiah . . .

(*The* SWITZERS *come to attention.* HADRIAN *enters up* R, *followed by* TALCRYN, COURTLEIGH, *another* CARDINAL, *and* FR ROSE. SANT *forgets himself and automatically makes to rise, then, remembering, sits down again insolently.* HADRIAN *assumes the throne.* RAGNA *moves behind the throne* L *of it.* FR ROSE *stands* R *of it and prepares to take notes on a clipboard.* TALACRYN *stands* R *of Rose, and the other* CARDINALS *take up positions* RC *and* LC. HADRIAN *makes a gesture dismissing the* SWISS GUARDS, *who, with the* CHAMBERLAINS, *exit up* R)

HADRIAN (*frigidly, but without menace*) We have summoned you in order that ye may speak your minds to Us. But Our utterances and yours shall be recorded. (*He indicates Rose*)

SANT. I object. This was to be a private interview.

HADRIAN. In order to start in a conciliatory mood, We concede. (*To Mrs Crowe*) Madam, what do you want?

MRS CROWE. Well, you know why I came here. I—er—I—er . . . (*She looks desperately to Sant for a lead*)

SANT. I think it would be more advantageous to all parties if I was to speak for Mrs. Crowe.

HADRIAN. We will concede this point also. Sir, we have received your questionable letter—are aware of your calumnies in the newspapers—and are now at a loss to know what more you could want of Us.

SANT (*rising*) Want? Well, I want reparation—damages, as you might say.

HADRIAN. For what?

SANT. Why, for the loss of time while I've had to be here, and for my business which I've been obliged to neglect while I've been kept waiting.

HADRIAN. To what extent have you suffered?

SANT. To what extent? (*Walking around below the throne*) Well, that shouldn't be difficult. I've been here since last July. Say eight months, and I generally allow a pound a day expenses. But it's cost me a sight more. You can add five hundred pounds for out-of-pockets. Then there's the business: say a year with salary and commission—call it three thousand. Then there's what we'll call damages (*significantly*) if you know what I mean. Well, including "damages" you might tot it all up together and call it—twenty thousand pounds.

HADRIAN. And your companion?

SANT. Well, better say double it. Forty thousand pounds spot cash in sterling and we'll cry quits.

(HADRIAN *takes a quick look round upon his* CARDINALS, *who return it*)

HADRIAN. You are demanding that We should pay you forty thousand pounds?

SANT (*sitting*) That's correct.

HADRIAN. Why do you demand this sum of Us?

SANT. Why? I should have thought I'd made my meaning plain. Do you want bells on it?

MRS. CROW (*obsequiously*) Perhaps if I could have a private word with His Holiness . . .

HADRIAN. Daughter, your notorious conduct debars you from a private conversation with any clergyman except in the open confessional.

MRS CROWE (*rising*) Oh, I see! So it's like that, is it? Well, I think you're going to regret what you've just said. Mr Sant was quite right about you. You must be shown up for what you really are. (*To Sant, as she sits*) Jerry, you tell him.

SANT (*to Mrs Crowe; gruffly*) Now just take it easy, will you? (*Rising, to Hadrian*) I'm afraid the lady is a wee bit upset, as well she might be. And I expect she is a wee bit embarrassed by the presence of so many people. Could we not dispense with those fine-looking gentlemen (*pointing to the Cardinals*) over there? (*He sits*)

HADRIAN (*to the Cardinals*) Your Eminences will be so good as to retire.

COURTLEIGH. Holiness, remember you are Sovereign within these walls.

RAGNA. I will tell the Chamberlains to take these people away.

HADRIAN. No. We thank your Lordships, but We are conducting this interview. Have no fears, since We have none.

(*The* CARDINALS *leave,* RAGNA *making gestures of despair.* FR ROSE *remains in the background*)

HADRIAN. And now . . .

SANT (*rising to* L *of the throne*) Now, sir, I should like to make an end to this matter and I daresay you've other things to be getting on with yourself. Suppose you make a suggestion. I don't think you'll find us unreasonable.

HADRIAN (*with deceptive mildness*) You ask that We should pay you forty thousand pounds—spot cash was the term you used—for damages which you say We have caused.

SANT. Aye, that's right.

HADRIAN. It's useless to point out to you that We did not ask you to waste your time in Rome?

SANT. In Rome! Not likely.

HADRIAN. And that we did not force you or induce you to neglect your business?

SANT (*getting angry*) No! But I daresay you were banking on it that I'd never dare face you, weren't ye? If ye'd have had the civility to have answered my letters and made an appointment like I suggested a while back, we'd have had this settled and done with without all this unpleasantness. (*He sits again*)

HADRIAN. For the credit of the human race, it must be said that indecent exhibitions of this kind are rare. But some men are gifted with an abnormal capacity for making fools of themselves. Mr Sant, does it not occur to you that you are engaging in foolish and singularly dirty business?

SANT (*leaping up*) Who d'ye think you're talking to? My hands are as clean as yours any day. Who skipped owing this lady here her rent, ay? Well, go on . . .

(HADRIAN *turns to* ROSE. FR ROSE *produces a receipt from the papers on his board, and moves down to Mrs Crowe, who disdains it with a shrug.* SANT *snatches it.* FR ROSE *returns upstage*)

HADRIAN. You know, Madam, that We paid this bill the moment we were in a position to do so.

SANT. Well, if you've paid her why shouldn't you pay me?

HADRIAN. Because We owe you nothing.

SANT. So that's the way of it. is it? Then, you'll be wanting to see a bit more about yer scabby little self in the papers then?

FR ROSE. Let me call the guard, Holiness.

HADRIAN (*signalling Fr Rose to remain quiet*) Listen, Mr Sant, We look upon you as a deeply injured man—

SANT (*sitting*) That's more like it.

HADRIAN —injured only by himself.

SANT. What?

HADRIAN. You have suffered loss and damage only because of your persistence in doing evil things. In this you have been your own enemy.

SANT (*rising*) Me own *what?* You sit there and tell me . . .

HADRIAN (*raising his voice*) Mr Sant, is it useless to ask you to change? You shall be helped. You will not be left alone.

SANT (*shouting*) I want what I come here to get—my money.

HADRIAN. If you wish honestly to earn a better living, We shall give you that opportunity.

SANT. The hell with that. What about damages for the past?

HADRIAN (*rising*) We promise you a chance for the future.

SANT (*with menace*) You won't pay, then?

HADRIAN. On your terms—not one farthing. But We will help you to save your soul.

SANT (*almost out of his mind*) You'll *save* my soul? You?

MRS CROWE (*urgently*) Jerry, sit down—please.

SANT (*to Hadrian*) You make me sick, you dirty Taigh.

MRS CROWE (*rising; desperately*) Jerry, I want to go. Please. It's no good.

SANT (*taking a step towards Hadrian*) He's just a little insect. Aren't ye?

MRS CROWE. Jerry, please . . .

FR ROSE (*running R in alarm*) Guard! *Presto! Presto!*

SANT (*quite out of his mind, moving down LC and drawing a revolver*) And ye know what to do with insects, don't ye? Tread them underfoot.

MRS CROWE (*shrieking*) Jerry!

(SWISS GUARDS, *not knowing what is required of them, rush in shouting "Pronto! Pronto!"*)

SANT. Vengeance is mine, Saith the Lord! Halleluya!

(*Before anyone can move,* SANT *fires once.* HADRIAN *stands quite still.* FR ROSE *rushes forward. The* GUARDS' *reactions are slower, but they follow.* SANT *fires for the second time, and* MRS CROWE *screams.* HADRIAN *remains still, though he seems to sway. As* SANT *fires for the third time,* FR ROSE *tries to interpose himself between Sant and Hadrian. He fails, but manages to catch Hadrian who now slowly subsides as a patch of crimson defiles the apostolic whiteness of his robe.* RAGNA, TALACRYN *and other* CARDINALS *rush in. The* GUARDS *overpower Sant, half killing him and holding him on the floor. The* CARDINALS *surround the throne. All eyes are turned to* HADRIAN *who is supported by* TALACRYN *on one side and* RAGNA *on the other. The* GUARDS *fling* SANT *on his knees before the dying Pope*)

HADRIAN (*weakly*) Father, forgive them for they know not—(*he struggles for breath*)—what they . . . Venerable Fathers, Our will and pleasure is . . .

TALACRYN. Speak it, Most Holy Father.

HADRIAN. Venerable Fathers, We name you all the ministers of
Our will. (*He turns towards Sant*) Son, you are forgiven. You are
free.

(SANT *is dragged off up* L *by the* GUARDS. *The hysterical* MRS CROWE
exits with him)

George, are you hurt? (*Unclasping his pectoral cross and giving it to
Fr Rose*) Dear Son, take this cross.

(FR ROSE *takes the cross and backs away* R, *weeping*. TALACRYN
and RAGNA *now beckon the others to support Hadrian's body and prepare
to administer final absolution. The room fills with Members of the
Sacred College and others*)

TALACRYN (*in a whisper; overcome with emotion*) The profession of
faith, Most Holy Lord.

HADRIAN. I believe all that which Holy Mother Church believes.
I ask pardon of all men. Dear Jesus, be not to me a judge but a
Saviour.

TALACRYN. Saints of God, advance to help him: Angels of the
Lord, come to meet him, receiving his soul, offering it in the Sight
of the Most High.

(HADRIAN *indicates his wish to be raised to his feet. He slowly
raises his right hand, which can hardly bear the weight of the two huge
Pontifical rings*)

HADRIAN. May God Omnipotent, (*the Sign of the Cross*) Father,
(*the Sign of the Cross*) Son, (*the Sign of the Cross*) and Holy Ghost,
bless you.

(HADRIAN *dies. A bell begins a solemn toll. Four* SWITZERS *lift up
Hadrian's body and carry it slowly round the stage and off up* L. *As they
do so, and the* CARDINALS *follow*, FR ROSE *moves down* C. *The* LIGHTS
gradually fade until only a spot is left on him)

FR ROSE (*as the body is being lifted and carried*) Prosit quaesumum,
Domine, animae famuli tui Frederick William Rolfe, Hadriane,
Summi Pontificis, misericordiae tuae implorata clementia; ut ejus,
in quo speravit et credidit, aeternum capiat, te miserante, con-
sortium. Per Dominum. (*He makes the Sign of the Cross*)

(*The two* CHAMBERLAINS *remove the throne and chairs, so that the
stage is now completely empty, except for* FR ROSE. *During the following,
a procession, led by acolytes with four candles, passes slowly across from
up* L *to up* R, *leading the bier of Hadrian*)

It had to happen. It was inevitable. By his own will he rejected
the beautiful solitude of peace in intellectual silence. Instead of
watching from the illimitable distance of his psychic altitude, by his
own wish he chose the inevitable certainty of ceaseless and ferocious
conflict among the ugly and obscene mob. It was the old bitter
feeling of disgust with himself that inspired him to do this, so
fearful was he that he might have seemed to be pleading for

sympathy. But he really had gone far, far beyond the realm of
human sympathy. There was not a man on earth who would have
dared to risk rebuff, to persist against rebuff, to soar to him with that
blessed salve of human sympathy for which—underneath his armour
—and behind his warlike mien—he yearned. Pity perhaps, horror
perhaps, dislike perhaps, might have met him. But he only empha-
sized his fastidious aloofness by disclosing the cold of marble, not
the warmth of human flesh. And so it happened. So died Hadrian
the Seventh, Bishop, Servant of the Servants of God—and maybe
Martyr.

(*As the end of the procession crosses,* ROLFE, *as he appeared at the
beginning of Act One, walks on from up* C *and watches with approval the
funeral cortège. He is smoking a cigarette and carries in his arms a huge
bundle of manuscript. The remaining* LIGHTS *start to fade*)

ROLFE   ⎫
FR ROSE   ⎬ (*in unison*) ⎰ Let us pray for the repose of his soul.
           ⎱ He was so tired.

The LIGHTS *fade to a*—

BLACKOUT

SCENE 8

SCENE—ROLFE'S *room in London at the beginning of Act One.*

When the LIGHTS *come up,* ROLFE *enters clutching his bundle of manuscript and moves to the fireplace. There is a knock on the door.*

MRS CROWE (*off*) Mr Rolfe!
ROLFE. What is it?

(MRS CROWE *enters*)

MRS CROWE. I came up to tell you that there's the two men
downstairs called to see you again.

(ROLFE *looks blank for a moment*)

ROLFE. What?
MRS CROWE (*with meaning*) You know.

(ROLFE *pauses in thought for a second*)

ROLFE (*eagerly*) Oh yes, of course. Their Lordships. Show them
up, please.
MRS CROWE (*dubiously*) Very well, then.

(MRS CROWE *exits.* ROLFE *puts the manuscript on the chair* C *and
tries to make himself look more respectable, then stands erect to receive
his visitors. In a minute they enter. It is the two* BAILIFFS. *The younger
holds a Warrant of Execution in his hand. The older smiles amiably*)

FIRST BAILIFF (*moving* C) Mr Corvo?
ROLFE (*scarcely audible*) No.
FIRST BAILIFF. Sorry, sir, *Baron* Corvo.
ROLFE (*icily*) That is not my name.
FIRST BAILIFF (*consulting his papers*) Of course, sir. You are Mr Frederick William Rolfe.

(ROLFE *stands erect but one knee begins to tremble. The* BAILIFFS *look round the room, appraising its pitiful contents with professional eyes*)

You were warned, Mr Rolfe. I did warn you, didn't I?

(ROLFE *stands rigid, saying nothing*)

Now I am afraid we shall be obliged to distrain your effects in accordance with this Warrant of Execution.

(*Still* ROLFE *says nothing*)

You do comprehend, don't you, Mr Rolfe, that we are acting with the authority of a Warrant issued by the Court?

(ROLFE *still remains silent and immobile*)

SECOND BAILIFF. A Warrant of Execution . . . (*He moves to the chair* C) I'm afraid this'll have to go too, sir.
FIRST BAILIFF. Mmm—yes. (*Looking suspiciously at the pile of manuscript*) Hadrian the Seventh. What's this then?
ROLFE (*picking up the manuscript and holding it to him*) A book.
SECOND BAILIFF (*piling books, and all small items onto the chest-of-drawers*) Write books, do you? (*He takes down the crucifix, the mirror and any other dressing and articles and puts them on the chest-of-drawers*)

(ROLFE *does not deign to answer*)

FIRST BAILIFF (*helping the other*) What's it about then?
ROLFE. About? It's about a man who made the fatuous and frantic mistake of living before his time.
FIRST BAILIFF. Any value?

(*The* SECOND BAILIFF *takes out the small chair and returns*)

ROLFE. It's a masterpiece and, therefore, probably not worth tuppence.

(*The two* BAILIFFS *exchange glances of incomprehension*)

At the same time, it is possibly beyond price. (*He passes his hands gently over the manuscript*)

(*The* BAILIFFS *look more than ever confused*)

FIRST BAILIFF (*to his colleague*) All right, then, let's get these out.

(*The* SECOND BAILIFF *takes out the* C *chair while the* FIRST *moves the chest-of-drawers round. The* SECOND BAILIFF *re-enters and between them they take out the chest-of-drawers.* ROLFE *stands quite still, holding his manuscript. After a moment the* FIRST BAILIFF *returns, moves to Rolfe, takes the manuscript, and goes to the door*)

FIRST BAILIFF. Best not to take any chances, Mr Rolfe. After all, you could be right.

(*The* FIRST BAILIFF *exits.* ROLFE *is lift all alone in the bare room, standing rigidly as he has done from the moment the bailiffs came in. As he stands there, one knee begins to tremble violently*)

CURTAIN

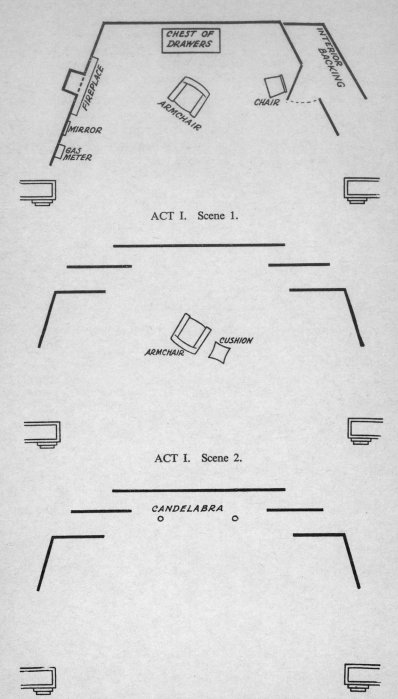

ACT I. Scene 1.

ACT I. Scene 2.

ACT I. Scene 3.

FURNITURE AND PROPERTY LIST

ACT I

SCENE 1

On stage: Wooden armchair (c). *On it:* rug, manuscript, pencil, blotting-paper
Small chair (L)
Chest-of-drawers (up c) *On top:* books, papers. *In drawers:* stiff
    collar, black tie, clothing
On mantelpiece: books, packet of oatmeal, cigarette papers and roller,
    tobacco, matches, pen
On wall down R; crucifix, mirror, gas meter
On floor down c: open bottle of ink
On floor up c: holdall.

Off stage: Papers on clipboard (FIRST BAILIFF)
Letter in envelope (MRS CROWE)
Tray with bowl of bread-and-milk, spoon, newspaper (AGNES)
Duster (AGNES)

Personal: ROLFE: handkerchief
AGNES: purse with coin
COURTLEIGH: sheet of paper (in breviary)
TALACRYN: wallet with £5 note

SCENE 2

On stage: Upright armchair (c)
Cushion (c)

Off stage: Stole (TALACRYN)

SCENE 3

On stage: Two candelabra (up RC and up LC)

Off stage: Tapers (ACOLYTES)
Incense, crosses, banners, Triple Crown on cushion (PROCESSIONALS)

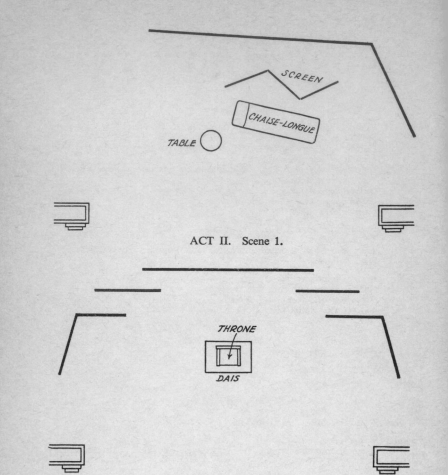

SCREEN

CHAISE-LONGUE

TABLE

ACT II.   Scene 1.

THRONE

DAIS

ACT II.   Scenes 2, 4, 6, 7.

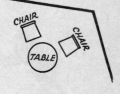

CHAIR

CHAIR

TABLE

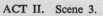

ACT II.   Scene 3.

ACT II

SCENE 1

On stage: Chaise-longue (LC). *On it:* newspaper (SANT)
        Screen (up LC)
        Table (C). *On it:* bottle of whiskey. 2 glasses
        (SANT, MRS CROWE)

SCENE 2

On stage: Throne on small dais (C)

Off stage: Bathchair (COURTLEIGH)
        Sheet of paper (ST ALBANS)
        Leather folder containing papers, press cuttings, ticket (HADRIAN)

SCENE 3

On stage: Small table (L)
        2 chairs (L)

Personal: Parasol (MRS CROWE)
        Piece of paper (SANT)

SCENE 4

On stage: Throne on small dais (C)

Off stage: Letter (TALACRYN)

Personal: HADRIAN: home-rolled cigarette

SCENE 5

On stage: Nil

SCENE 6

On stage: Throne on small dais (C)
        Small chair (down RC)

Off stage: Clip of papers, with card and pen (ROSE)
        Handbag with packet of money and jar of pickles (AGNES)
        Newspapers (RAGNA)
        Parasol (ROSE)

SCENE 7

Set: Chair from R of throne to down RC
        Second chair down LC

Off stage: Clipboard with receipt, papers and pen (ROSE)
        Revolver (SANT)
        Candles (ACOLYTES)
        Bier
        Bundle of manuscript (ROLFE)

Personal: SANT: loose change

SCENE 8

On stage: Furniture and properties as Act I Scene 1, except for tray, bowl,
        rug and ink-bottle

Off stage: Bundle of manuscript (ROLFE)
        Warrant of Execution (FIRST BAILIFF)

EFFECTS PLOT

ACT I

SCENE 1

No cues

SCENE 2

Cue 1	TALACRYN: "... travel together, Freddy" *Bell tolls and Liturgy is sung.* *Continue through change*	(page 18)

SCENE 3

Cue 2	ROLFE and TALACRYN enter *Stop bell and Liturgy*	(page 19)
Cue 3	ROLFE: "... have insisted that ..." *Bell tolls*	(page 20)
Cue 4	After general entrance *Bell stops*	(page 20)
Cue 5	ROLFE: "I will" *Organ peals out*	(page 21)

ACT II

SCENE 1

No cues

SCENE 2

No cues

SCENE 3

No cues

SCENE 4

No cues

SCENE 5

Cue 6	At start of scene *Distant bell rings*	(page 34)
Cue 7	When Procession exits *Bell stops*	(page 34)

SCENE 6

No cues

SCENE 7

Cue 8	As HADRIAN dies *Bell tolls*	(page 50)
Cue 9	When funeral cortege exits *Bell stops*	(page 51)

SCENE 8

No cues

LIGHTING PLOT

Apart from the gas-fire in Act I, no property fittings are required throughout. No specific times of day nor apparent sources of light need be indicated.

ACT I SCENE 1

To open:	Bring up general lighting	
Cue 1	AGNES lights fire	(page 6)
	Bring up gas-fire effect	
Cue 2	ROLFE starts writing	(page 8)
	Change lighting to warmer hue	
Cue 3	ROLFE exists	(page 15)
	Fade to Blackout	

ACT I SCENE 2

Cue 4	When ready	(page 15)
	Bring up general lighting	
Cue 5	TALACRYN: "... travel together, Freddy	(page 18)
	Fade to Blackout	

ACT I SCENE 3

Cue 6	When ready	(page 19)
	Bring up general lighting	

ACT II SCENE 1

To open:	Bring up general lighting.	
Cue 7	SANT kisses Mrs Growe	(page 24)
	Fade to Blackout	

ACT II SCENE 2

Cue 8	When ready	(page 25)
	Bring up general lighting	
Cue 9	HADRIAN and COURTLEIGH exit	(page 32)
	Fade to Blackout	

ACT II SCENE 3

Cue 10	When ready	(page 32)
	Bring up general lighting	
Cue 11	SANT: "... should be made good"	(page 32)
	Fade to Blackout	

ACT II SCENE 4

Cue 12	When ready	(page 33)
	Bring up general lighting	
Cue 13	TALACRYN and HADRIAN exit	(page 34)
	Fade to Blackout	

ACT II SCENE 5

Cue 14   When ready   (page 34)
            Bring up general lighting

Cue 15   HADRIAN: ". . . will pass for Love"   (page 38)
            Fade to Blackout

ACT II SCENE 6

Cue 16   When ready   (page 38)
            Bring up general lighting

Cue 17   HADRIAN and RAGNA exit   (page 45)
            Fade to Blackout

ACT II SCENE 7

Cue 18   When ready   (page 46)
            Bring up general lighting

Cue 19   HADRIAN's body is carried off   (page 50)
            Fade to spot down C

Cue 20   Procession exits   (page 51)
            Fade to Blackout

ACT II SCENE 8

Cue 21   When ready   (page 51)
            Bring up to same lighting as start of play

PRINTED IN GREAT BRITAIN BY BUTLER & TANNER LTD, FROME AND LONDON